WEL
HOMETO

Twelve uniqu

Where you can find romance and adventure, bachelors and babies, feuding families, a case of mistaken identity, and a mum on the run!

Join us in America's favourite town and experience the love and the laughter, the trials and the triumphs of those who call it home.

*First published in Great Britain 2000
by Harlequin Mills & Boon Limited,
Eton House, 18-24 Paradise Road,
Richmond, Surrey TW9 1SR*

PUPPY LOVE © Harlequin Books S.A. 1996

Ginger Chambers is acknowledged as the author of this work.

ISBN 0 373 82558 7

110-0900

*Printed and bound in Spain
by Litografia Rosés S.A., Barcelona*

GINGER CHAMBERS

Puppy Love

TORONTO • NEW YORK • LONDON
AMSTERDAM • PARIS • SYDNEY • HAMBURG
STOCKHOLM • ATHENS • TOKYO • MILAN • MADRID
PRAGUE • WARSAW • BUDAPEST • AUCKLAND

WELCOME TO A
HOMETOWN REUNION

**Twelve books set in Tyler.
Twelve unique stories.**

Romance novels were **Ginger Chambers**'s favourite escape when her children were small, and when she decided to try her hand at writing a book, it was a romance. That was more than twenty years and many, many books ago. She's a long-time resident of San Francisco who says visiting Tyler for a Hometown Reunion was like coming home again—revisiting friends and neighbours, catching up on all the latest goings-on. 'It reminds me,' she says, 'of my large family, all the cousins and aunts and uncles getting together after time apart. What fun!'

CHAPTER ONE

GRACIE LAWSON GRITTED her teeth and did what she had to do. She pinned a friendly smile on her face and stepped through the doorway into the hotel lobby.

There was no way to get around what was coming. She'd known it since first making the commitment. *It will be good for me,* she told herself for the thousandth time in the last six weeks. And for the thousandth time her knees quivered.

It was still very early in the morning, and the majority of the guests at Timberlake Lodge had yet to stir. Only the first of the behind-the-scenes workers of the dog show had started to assemble. Like her, most were from the surrounding area and were commuting from their homes.

"Gracie, hi! Over here!" a woman called, waving from across the lobby.

Gracie approached the small group of people.

"You haven't talked with Diane this morning, have you?" someone asked.

"Diane? No," Gracie replied.

"She was supposed to be here a half hour ago to meet with Eileen, and she hasn't…"

The elevator doors opened and a nicely dressed couple stepped out. Gracie saw them, then looked away quickly, her heart pounding. The man nearest her continued to talk, but Gracie no longer followed his words. She was aware only of Raymond and Claudette Wilson walking toward them and then, barely a few steps away, veering off down the hall that led to the restaurant. They hadn't seen her!

Raymond and Claudette...Paul's closest friends and fellow dog handlers. She hadn't seen them in the last year and a half, not since she'd stopped attending competitions. Not since the last time she'd put in an appearance and been the object of such pity.

That was the main problem about being part of a tightly knit world. Everyone knew everyone else, and when something bad happened, it got around. Tyler's gossips had nothing on the regulars of the dog-show circuit. Particularly when the "something bad" involved a well-known breeder and one of the top dog handlers in the country.

"Oh! Here she comes! Here she comes! Diane!" Relieved exclamations burst from the people around Gracie.

Diane Jennings strode across the lobby to join them, her square, rather plain face beaming good-naturedly. "Sorry I'm late," she said. "A last-minute panic at home. Has everyone had breakfast who wants it? Since many of you are novices to large competitions, I'll warn you now—it's going to be a long time until lunch! Gracie can verify that." She sent a huge smile toward Gracie.

"That's right," Gracie agreed, trying to speak around the lump in her throat.

She wished she hadn't agreed to do this! She

wasn't ready yet. Not that it would be the full com-
plement of competitors. This was a regional specialty
show sponsored by the Sugar Creek Poodle Club and
was for poodles only. It wasn't an all-breed show,
where she would be in danger of running into Paul.
If that had been a possibility, she wouldn't have…

She jumped when Diane Jennings, the club's president, touched her arm. The others had moved off,
eager to take up their assignments.

Diane looked at her, her expression serious. "If
you don't want to do this, Gracie, don't. I understand."

"No, it's all right. *I'm* all right."

Diane sighed. "You shouldn't be the one to hide
away. It wasn't your fault. It was his."

"It was a misunderstanding," Gracie said tightly.
"Anyway, it's been two years."

Before Diane could say anything more, one of her
minions returned to claim her. "Diane, I need you to
tell me again…"

Gracie used the interruption to break away. She
hurried back across the lobby and slipped gratefully
into the nicely appointed women's room she knew
was there from her weeks of preliminary work helping to coordinate the competition.

Just her luck, she thought, she'd probably run into
Sheilie. And she'd have to make up some kind of
explanation to her niece about why she looked so
shaken. But the room was empty except for a desk
clerk, who smiled distractedly at her before hurrying
back to her post.

Gracie slumped into one of the chintz-covered

chairs in the powder area and waited for her nerves to calm down.

Sheilie didn't know about Paul. Not by name. Gracie had told her only that she'd been involved with someone for a number of years and that two years ago they'd parted. She hadn't told her why, or that it had come as much of a shock to her as it had to the rest of the dog-show world. Sheila would probably learn more if she overheard any of the circuit regulars talking, but there was an equal chance she wouldn't hear a thing. Hotel managers were usually kept busy running the hotel.

A short time later Gracie made herself go to the mirror, where she straightened her skirt and blouse and lightly fluffed her short blond hair. She could still see the strain in her face, but once again she forced herself to smile, and the change was miraculous. She looked bright and happy and completely in control.

From the moment she'd heard that Raymond and Claudette were scheduled to attend the event—poodles were their specialty—she'd been bracing herself to see them, to talk to them. They were nice people. But their loyalty, naturally, went to Paul.

Paul…who'd shocked her into near seclusion two years before when he'd announced his elopement with the young woman who only three years earlier had won the top showmanship title for junior handlers. And who, at nineteen, was less than half his age.

By now it should have stopped hurting.

By now Gracie should be able to go out there and

meet anyone—even Paul and Jessica!—with her head held high and a gleam of confidence in her eye.

But it still hurt, and she found it difficult to produce a gleam of any kind, much less in-your-face confidence.

Until recently she'd felt completely adrift. Then she'd made a big decision and had followed it immediately with another. Her world was finally starting to shift.

To aid in that shift, she'd agreed, when asked, to act as liaison between the hotel and the poodle club. It would be good for her, she'd told herself. *Good for her!*

She repeated the words into the mirror, then, straightening her shoulders, went back to the lobby.

"AH-CHOO! *Ah-choo!*"

Angus Watson wiped his stubby nose with a large handkerchief and swore miserably beneath his breath. His eyes were streaming, his nose was running, his skin itched. And all because of those damned dogs. They were everywhere! He'd taken double the dosage of antihistamines recommended on the box, and the only result so far had been a fuzzy mind. He'd have gone to sleep in the elevator while descending from his room to the lobby if he hadn't been trapped inside it with one of those fancy-cut furry rats that were making his life such a misery. And with the proud owner.

"Don Juan," the woman cooed into the tiny animal's ear. "You're the best poodle in the competition, aren't you, baby? And you're going to win top prize for Mommy, too, aren't you? Isn't that right?''

Disgusting.

Angus stuffed the handkerchief back into his pocket as he headed for the front desk. Barks accompanied his every step. Don Juan had been set upon his little feet and was now yapping happily at his owner's heels as she crossed the lobby to the front doors. Several other poodles, large to small, were also in the lobby with their owners and took up their compatriot's cause. All were restrained by leashes, but that was little comfort to Angus.

''Ah-choo! Ahh-chooo!'' He exploded again, making another grab for his handkerchief.

He marched up to the raised oak counter and, ignoring the fact that the clerk was already speaking to someone, demanded shortly, ''I want to speak with the manager. Right now, this very minute! You tell him—'' His words were interrupted by another loud sneeze.

The two women, one on either side of the desk, looked at each other, then back at him. The one who stood in his way stepped aside to allow him full access.

''It's criminal!'' Angus bellowed, moving forward. ''I pay good money for a pleasant vacation and look what happens.'' He waved the balled-up handkerchief at the numerous dogs, only to jerk his hand back to scratch his other arm, then the side of his neck, then a barely accessible spot in the middle of his back. ''The manager!'' he thundered. ''At once!''

"I'm the manager, sir," the tall, slender blonde behind the desk volunteered.

Angus raised himself to his full five feet, five inches. If he hadn't been feeling so awful he might have had a little fun. A bombastic performance would be right in keeping with the persona he'd assumed. As it was, he meant every word. "I want these…these *beasts*…out of the hotel. What were you thinking of, to allow them here in the first place? It's an assault on the health and welfare of every registered guest! Look at me. Look!" With perfect timing, he sneezed violently again.

The manager's brow furrowed. "Is there anything we can do to help you, sir? Call a doctor? A pharmacist?"

"I don't need a doctor or more pills!" he shouted. "Get rid of the dogs!"

"It's a dog show, sir. And it's been scheduled for months."

"I don't care if it's been scheduled for years! I came to relax, play a little golf…"

"The dogs are restricted to certain areas…"

"That they're here at all is enough!"

The woman who'd given up her space at the counter spoke up. "Actually, poodles are recommended for people who have allergies. They don't shed, they don't have dog dander. Their hair is similar to human hair."

Angus turned on her. She was shorter than he was by a number of inches, petite yet very nicely curved— something he'd been too distracted to notice earlier. She also was quite pretty in a woman-over-thirty sort of way, with her short blond hair and her lively brown eyes. Just the kind of female who'd usually appeal to him...if it hadn't been for his allergies.

He glared at her and demanded incredulously, "Are you trying to tell me that the way I feel is all in my head?"

Her smile was warm enough to melt steel. "No, just that most people aren't allergic. Obviously, you are." She extended her hand. "My name is Gracie Lawson. I'm the liaison for the poodle club sponsoring the event."

Her skin was soft, pleasingly feminine. In spite of himself Angus's irritation began to dissolve.

"I'm sorry you're having a problem, Mr...?"

"Watson. Angus Watson," Angus supplied gruffly.

"The competition lasts for two days, Mr. Watson. Today and tomorrow. Then we'll be gone."

The manager's fingers flew over a keyboard. "A possible solution might be to transfer you to another room, Mr. Watson." She gazed intently at a video monitor. "You've been with us for two weeks and plan to stay for two more, correct?"

"Yes," Angus agreed.

"Would you be willing to move to another wing? One where there are no dogs? Your room would be upgraded as well. It's a suite, actually. And you'd still be charged the original rate."

"For two days?" Angus demanded.

The manager smiled. "No, for the remainder of your stay."

Angus sniffed. "And there'd be no dogs?"

"None at all, sir."

For the first time since his allergies had started to attack him, Angus's round cheeks creased in a smile. "That would be very nice," he said. "I'd like that."

The manager clicked a few more keys and the deed was done, and by a further miracle of modern technology, a moment later Angus was handed the magnetic key card that was his entry into an even finer world.

Damn, he liked the perks of this job, he thought. Timberlake Lodge was a classy place to stay. Far better than the jail cells his other accomplices had been stuck in before Celeste Huntington had sent her lawyer to spring them free. Now Angus was going to luxuriate in a suite! And Celeste Huntington couldn't complain, because he was getting it at a bargain rate!

She was a funny woman, Celeste Huntington. She was willing to go to any lengths to gain possession of her grandchild, not caring much whether they were within the law or not. But she didn't want her paid help to be too comfortable while they did her dirty work.

Take him, for example. Since he alone of her henchmen had escaped the failed attempt to snatch the child, she'd ordered him to put up at Timberlake Lodge. He didn't have to worry about being recognized; no one knew his face or his name. His assignment was to learn all he could about where the quarry they'd flushed out might have escaped to. But he'd better not run up the tab. Otherwise Celeste would have his head on a stick to show to anyone else who might entertain similar notions.

That was why it was so eminently satisfying to be

handed something for free. To get at her, as well as to satisfy his own bent for larceny.

Recalling himself to the moment, Angus excused himself to the two women by bowing from the waist, then started back to his room to pack. When he was ready, he'd call for a bellman to assist him in his move. Yes, this was definitely the life!

He didn't realize until it was too late that he was once again fated to share the elevator with Don Juan. As the doors slid silently shut, the little white dog, held tightly in his owner's arms, started its yappy bark, and Angus couldn't help but wish that it wouldn't blow his cover if he gave its neck a quick twist.

GRACIE AND SHEILA watched Angus Watson disappear into the elevator and heard the resounding sneeze that immediately followed.

"What a strange little man," Gracie murmured.

"He certainly jumped at the chance for a suite."

"Wouldn't you?" Gracie challenged her niece dryly. "By the way, does he always dress like that?"

"Hasn't missed a day since he checked in. He looks like he stepped right off the last hole at St. Andrews—plus fours, argyle socks, tweed jacket and usually a cap."

"A traditional golfing enthusiast."

"Word's come back from someone who played a round with him that he's awful! No ability whatsoever."

"Even stranger," Gracie said.

"I'm relieved he was so easy to pacify."

"You handled the situation perfectly, Sheilie."

"As did you." The younger woman's smile turned mischievous. "I think he was attracted to you. I saw his face light up for a second in between sneezes."

Gracie rolled her eyes. "Give it a rest, okay? I'm not interested."

"That's what you always say."

Gracie wanted to turn the conversation away from herself. Most times she could join in with her niece's teasing and even tease back, but not today. She was under too much strain. "I don't seem to remember you being in much of a hurry to find a man before you met Douglas."

"Ahh, but you have to agree, Douglas is different. He—"

Sheila broke off as a commotion started just inside the hotel's main entrance. Two toy poodles had gotten free from their owner and, trailing their leashes, run to greet a new arrival.

The woman—a vision of elegance in pure silk and soft black leather, her expensively styled, honey-blond hair perfectly in place, her skin a glowing advertisement for all the elixirs applied during a lifetime of pampering—stood transfixed. She seemed of two minds whether to scream or to laugh as the dogs frolicked around her ankles, pawing at her hose and barking excitedly.

Sheila give a strangled squeak, but before Gracie could turn to her, the woman under siege began to laugh. Her laugh tinkled and trilled as she dropped to one knee to return the dogs' greetings.

"*Lady Holmes!*" Sheila whispered tightly.

An amazing collection of monogrammed luggage filled the arms of several bellmen. Wide-eyed, Gracie looked from the luggage to the woman, who was now making a great show of petting the little dogs. She didn't seem to mind that their paws might be ruining her clothing. Her smile was as beneficent as an angel's.

"Mr. Wocheck is going to fire me for this!" Sheila moaned as she freed herself from her frozen state and hurried out from behind the desk.

"Lady Holmes…I'm so sorry," she apologized as she waded into the fray.

Lady Holmes straightened when the owner finally resumed control of his animals. "It's perfectly all right," she said, dismissing Sheila's apology in a cultured, slightly accented voice. "I love dogs, particularly poodles. I had one—a silver one—when I was a child."

Sheila ushered the woman across the lobby to the front desk. "Is Mr. Wocheck expecting you?" she asked, then turned to murmur something to the desk clerk, who in turn nodded crisply and reached for the telephone.

"He knows of my plans," Lady Holmes replied. "But not the time of my arrival."

"I've sent word to him that you're here, Lady Holmes."

The woman Gracie knew only by reputation nodded. She was as lovely as Gracie had heard and as beautifully kept. No expense had been spared, from perfume to perfect lip shade. Lady Nicole Holmes, spoiled socialite, held an array of connections to the power behind Addison Hotels International. She was daughter of the founder of the worldwide chain. Her son, Devon Addison, was running the company now, and her ex-husband, Edward Wocheck, remained president. A woman of strong will and impetuous nature, she had recently divorced her third husband, a member of the British aristocracy.

Gracie was treated to a sweep of the woman's huge, gray-green eyes, and for a moment she felt like a moth pinned in an exhibit. Her lack of eminence soon became apparent, though, and the inspection ended.

Gracie couldn't help it; she smiled. It was her first genuine experience of levity that day.

Within seconds a tall, distinguished-looking man strode into view.

"Edward," Lady Holmes murmured with satisfaction.

"Nikki!" he returned, taking her hands. "I didn't expect you this soon."

A tiny frown marred Lady Holmes's perfect face. "I couldn't wait. Hawaii became a prison for me the instant I learned of Devon's plans." She gave light pecks to both of her ex-husband's cheeks. Whether from habit or strained nerves, when she pulled back she ignored the fact that they were not alone. "You must talk to him, Edward!" she pleaded. "Right away! Make him see how foolhardy it is for him to follow Kathleen Kelsey into that terrible place! He'll listen to you!"

Edward Wocheck, mindful of the people around them, placed an arm around Lady Holmes's delicate shoulders and urged her forward. "Let's go to your suite, Nikki," he said. "We can discuss it there."

The beautiful blond head rested lightly against his jacket for a moment before lifting regally. "But you're the person who has had the most influence in making him what he is today, aren't you?" she said as they moved away. "You'd do the same thing, wouldn't you? Rush in and play the hero, no matter what the danger…"

Her words faded as they progressed across the lobby toward the west wing.

Once they were gone Sheila released a pent-up breath. Then she said softly, "Personally, I'm glad he's going. Johnny and Anna have been so worried about Kathleen."

Gracie shook her head. She didn't know anything about Johnny and Anna Kelsey being worried about their youngest daughter. The last she'd heard, Kathleen had been working for Edward Wocheck as his executive assistant, traveling with him to exciting places around the globe.

Sheila sighed. "Maybe it *is* a good thing you sold the kennel. You're so out of touch! I worried at first that selling it was a mistake—you've given so much of yourself to it for so long. But maybe you gave *too* much. Particularly the last year or—"

"Bring me up to speed," Gracie interrupted, not wanting to get into a discussion about these last two years.

"Let's go to my office," Sheila said.

Gracie checked her watch. "I only have a few minutes before I have to meet Diane."

"This won't take long."

In the office, which was decorated with her niece's usual good taste, Sheila waved her into a chair and said, "Kathleen's in Yugoslavia...or rather, a tiny section of what used to be Yugoslavia. Don't ask me why. All I know is Johnny and Anna are worried sick because they haven't heard from her. And Devon Addison...you know who he is, don't you?" Gracie nodded. "Well, Devon is going in after her, to try to find her and bring her out!"

"Why him?" Gracie asked.

Sheila shrugged. "Who knows? To be a hero, like his mother said?"

"Are they close?"

"I'm only the manager here. All I know is he's planning to go and his mother doesn't like it. Not one tiny little bit."

"I can't say I blame her. She's afraid for him." Gracie checked her watch again. "My meeting with Diane," she murmured.

Sheila frowned. "I think I'll call Glenna tonight and see if her parents have heard anything new."

"Let me know if they have, okay?"

Sheila walked with her to the door. "Why don't you have dinner with Douglas and me this evening? We're making lasagna."

"Sounds tempting, but I've promised to meet some friends."

"Dog-show people?"

"Naturally."

"I thought that's why you sold the kennel—to get away from having your life dominated by dogs."

"If it gives you any satisfaction, I'd rather have dinner with you and Douglas."

Sheila looked at her closely. "You do look a little frazzled around the edges."

"Why, thank you…and you look nice, too!" Gracie's favorite defense was a dry quip. Her niece had no idea of the strain she was under, and Gracie was determined that it remain that way.

Sheila laughed. "I didn't mean it like that! I meant… Oh, you know what I meant. I was just wondering if you were okay."

"I'm fine. As happy as a lark meeting old friends and renewing acquaintances."

"Then why would you rather have dinner with Douglas and me?"

Gracie pretended to concede defeat. "All right. You caught me out. I lied."

"Now why don't I believe that?" Sheila mused.

Gracie hurried down the hall, seemingly intent upon keeping her appointment. In reality, she was evading having to answer any more uncomfortable questions from her niece.

Only ten years separated the two of them in age, but instead of growing up close, as would be expected of two members of a small family in a small town, they mostly had been estranged. Gracie's half brother and Sheila's father, Emil, had been thirty-three years old when Gracie was born. He was the product of their father's first marriage, she the product of his second. After their father's death, when Gracie was nine, she and her mother had moved into town, and

Emil, newly married, had taken over running the family dairy farm.

Because emotions had been strained between stepmother and stepson, Gracie's visits to the farm had been infrequent. She remembered going back on occasion; she remembered the day Sheila was born. But the bond that might ordinarily have existed between the two girls had never flowered. They'd only become really close over the past year, brought together by their mutual concern over Emil's state of health. Sheila's leaving her job in Chicago to move back to Tyler had helped their friendship, and more recently Gracie's own return to their hometown.

It was strange how an occurrence in one life could create ripples that spread through a number of others. Like a pebble tossed into a still pond, the rings moved outward in ever-increasing circles. Myrna Lawson's long and losing battle with a terrible illness, Emil's deep depression, Sheila's fear that she might lose her father, too… Gracie and Paul falling in love, their years-long relationship, everyone's expectation that one day they would marry. Paul meeting Jessica, Paul and Jessica secretly marrying, Gracie's subsequent withdrawal to the kennel. Sheila moving back to Tyler to be with her father, and her meeting Douglas Wagner again… All were circles within circles, continuing to expand.

Gracie hadn't wanted to go into detail when her niece probed gently into the reasons why she remained unmarried at nearly forty. Sheila had claimed she couldn't understand it, since Gracie was still quite pretty, with a great shape and an engaging personality.

A quick wit and clever tongue had given Gracie cover. She'd provided a brief account of her recent past, glossing over the many layers of hurt.

She was off men now, she'd declared. She was proud, she was independent, she was alone…and that was the way she wanted it.

And Sheila had believed her.

CHAPTER TWO

GRACIE FOUND Diane Jennings inside the large banquet room that had been converted into a judging area. The room was abuzz with activity. Helpers and officials were fussing over the awards table, giving a last-minute polish to the trophies and arranging the ribbons to best advantage, reattaching a fallen banner, repositioning a spray of flowers that had been moved out of place. The ring steward was checking the order of competitors listed on his clipboard. Meanwhile a crowd had started to gather.

Diane spotted Gracie and beamed. "It was a stroke of genius to hold the competition at Timberlake, Gracie. The lodge couldn't be a better venue. Everyone I've talked to has been so impressed. Not only are the facilities beautiful—absolutely beautiful!—but the people who work here have been wonderful, too. The committee is *so* pleased!"

"I can't believe the number of entries," Gracie said.

"Have you seen the grooming area?" Diane asked. "You have to emphasize to your niece how much we appreciate all the trouble everyone has taken."

"I will."

"You are planning to come to the lunch for the

judges, aren't you? We have a place reserved for you.''

''I wasn't sure you'd want me to, since I'm not showing this year.''

''Don't be silly!'' Diane exclaimed. ''You've worked so hard to insure the success of the show. Of course we want you!''

Someone rushed up and pulled on Gracie's elbow, bubbling over in greeting. ''Gracie Lawson, as I live and breathe! I was hoping I'd see you! Honey, how *are* you?'' Gracie turned to see Barbara Egan, a tall, thin fellow breeder and a whirlwind from the state of Texas. ''It's been so long!'' Barbara cried, hugging her. ''How have you been? Have you seen my miniature bitch yet? I'm really having a lot of luck with her this year. She's won her breed in her last three shows!''

The rush of questions and information was typical of Barbara. Gracie hugged her back. ''I'm fine, and no, I haven't seen your bitch yet. I haven't had a chance.''

In the background the first of the competitions was starting to get underway as the puppies were called into the show ring.

''What's this I hear about you selling Grace Farms?'' Barbara demanded. ''That was just a rumor, wasn't it? Tell me it's not true.''

Gracie could sense that others ears around them were listening. She started to reply, but Barbara added, ''It's not because of Paul and Jessica, is it? I mean, you wouldn't sell your kennel because—''

''No, it wasn't that,'' Gracie assured her quickly.

"That was two years ago. I—I'm not silly enough to—"

"Well, good!" Barbara declared. "I didn't think you were. There isn't a man on the planet worth doing something like that for. Particularly Paul. I mean, really, the man's a cad!"

Gracie felt her cheeks turn pink. In order to divert attention from her reaction, she took up where her friend left off. "An absolute cur!" she agreed.

"A *scoundrel!*" Barbara exclaimed. Then she started to laugh. "Honestly, I thought he'd get himself arrested for robbing the cradle!"

Gracie laughed with her, even though she'd far rather have cried. The only way to get through these moments and those that were sure to follow, she'd decided, was to make light of the whole thing. To demonstrate that she was no longer that hurting mass of protoplasm that had crept away early from the last show she'd attended.

Barbara and a number of others had stood up for her and condemned Paul. But somehow that had made the situation worse, pitting friend against friend.

"You've still kept Jacques and Hortense, of course," Barbara said. "And Jo-Jo." She named the champion toy poodles that Gracie had shown for years as an owner-breeder-handler.

"Of course. Only…Hortense died."

"Oh, I'm sorry," Barbara murmured.

Gracie shrugged, a simple motion that belied the memory of her sorrow earlier in the year when she'd lost her beloved bitch.

"Aren't you showing either of the boys here?" Barbara asked.

Gracie shook her head. "No, I'm not doing that now, either. I haven't since…" She stopped when she realized that what she'd been about to reveal was in direct contradiction to her earlier statement.

But she needn't have worried about Barbara picking up on anything. Her friend's attention had been caught by what was happening in the ring. "Oh, look!" she cried, grinning and pointing. "Isn't he something? He thinks he owns the place!"

Gracie looked around in time to see a tiny toy-poodle pup in the six-to-nine-month class being guided around the ring by his handler. Little more than a bit of white fur, he moved with the confidence of a natural-born champion.

Gracie, too, started to smile, then for some reason she glanced up…into the fixed gaze of a man who stood on the opposite side of the show ring.

His quizzical gaze remained steadily on her.

Why was he looking at her like that? Gracie wondered. Then his smile broadened and he winked…and she realized after a shocked moment that he was flirting with her. With her!

Gracie turned away swiftly. How ridiculous!

Barbara touched her arm and said something more about the puppy. But Gracie had a hard time ignoring the tingling sensation between her shoulder blades. She was sure he was still watching her.

Yet when she ventured another look, being careful not to do it in such a way as to draw attention, he was gone. He might have been a figment of her imagination.

As Barbara continued to talk, moving back to the subject of Gracie's kennel and her dismay about its sale, she didn't seem to notice that Gracie had a hard time focusing.

THE LARGE, wood-paneled dining room at Timberlake Lodge was filled with people. Gracie moved through their midst, forcing herself to smile at familiar faces. Occasionally someone stopped her to ask if she'd like to join their table. Gracie was relieved to be able to refuse. If she could do as she wanted, she wouldn't be here right now at all. She'd be off somewhere alone, trying to regroup for the afternoon session. But Diane's request that she share the table reserved for the officials and judges of the competition had been made from the heart and was intended as an honor. Gracie couldn't refuse.

"There you are!" Diane said as she arrived at the oversize round table positioned where the occupants would have a good view of the grounds. "We'd almost given up on you!"

Gracie slipped into the remaining empty chair. "A small problem cropped up," she said.

"A problem?" Diane repeated, instantly concerned.

Gracie wrinkled her nose. "It's all been taken care of. Nothing to worry about." She gave a short greeting to her luncheon companions on either side. The middle-aged woman to her left was an impeccably credentialed judge who'd only recently moved to the

Midwest from southern California; the man on her right was a representative of the American Kennel Club.

"Gracie Lawson, everyone," Diane said, introducing her to the table at large. "For those of you who don't already know her, Gracie is the person responsible for helping us secure our wonderful accommodations. And it's also due to her many hours of hard work in preparation that the competition is running so smoothly."

Diane's praise was followed by a muted round of applause, both of which made Gracie squirm. "Thank you," she murmured.

Conversation resumed around the table. The judge on Gracie's left asked her if she was a local resident. When Gracie confirmed that she was, the woman rushed into an array of questions about Tyler and the surrounding countryside. Were winter sports popular here, particularly cross-country skiing? Were the courses challenging? Was it difficult to book into the lodge in December?

Gracie answered as best she could, but not being a winter-sports enthusiast, she couldn't tell her about the courses. Whereupon the person sitting on the other side of the judge leaned forward to say, "I couldn't help overhearing...."

Gracie blinked. It was him! The same young man who had winked at her earlier!

"We have some of the finest cross-country skiing areas in the region," he continued, his tone helpful and friendly. "For years we managed to keep it our little secret, but now the secret is out. If you're wanting to stay at the lodge in December, you should make your reservations early. It can get pretty crowded.''

Who *was* he? Gracie wondered. He spoke like a local, but he didn't look like anyone she had ever met before. He had fine, even features, a squarish jaw and golden brown eyes. Eyes that now showed amusement at her startled reaction. Any number of new people had moved into the Tyler area while she'd been devoting herself to the kennel, though. Especially during the last two years, when she'd been in such a funk....

''Why thank you, Dr. Phelps,'' the woman said brightly, as she turned to him. ''I didn't realize you were from the Tyler area. But then I should have, shouldn't I, since you're with the local poodle club?''

''Not exactly 'with,''' he murmured.

Phelps...Phelps... Gracie repeated the name in her mind. The only Phelpses she knew were members of the George Phelps family. Or, she amended, what used to be a family. Dr. George Phelps once had been chief of staff at Tyler General Hospital. Recently, he'd handed over those reins to Jeff Baron and had semiretired—just as he had retired from his first marriage, to quickly enter a second with Marge Peterson, owner of Marge's Diner.

Gracie smiled to herself. Sheila would be proud that she'd put together that much Tyler gossip. She leaned forward for a better look at the handsome young doctor. There was only one young male Phelps that she knew of...Roger. Her brow furrowed. What was it she had last heard about him? Something about him leaving the medical school he was attending in New York?

He caught her gaze and winked again. He actually winked—in front of everyone!

Gracie jerked back. Why was he doing this? She chanced a quick glance at the other people around the table and saw that no one had noticed. Relieved, she buried her nose in her menu.

It was impossible not to hear most of the conversation that took place between the judge and Dr. Phelps as lunch progressed. The judge, it seemed, saw absolutely nothing wrong with a flagrant flirtation. She spoke exclusively to him and laughed at anything even remotely clever that he said.

Gracie kept her gaze glued to her plate. Such an outward display made her uncomfortable. She refused to look to her left.

When the meal finally ended Gracie jumped up, ready to make a quick getaway. But Diane stopped her, pulling her aside. "I was wondering, Gracie," the president of the poodle club said in a low voice, "would you mind taking charge of Dr. Phelps for a bit? He's far too much of a gentleman to complain, but I don't think he appreciates all the attention Mrs. Wilcox is giving him."

"He didn't seem very displeased to me," Gracie said tightly.

"He was just being polite. It was embarrassing the way she latched on to him. And all that coquettish laughter. Doesn't she realize how ridiculous that looks in a woman her age?" Diane shook her head. "Could you help us out? Please?"

"I'm very busy, Diane," Gracie answered.

"It's only for an hour, then Mrs. Wilcox will be safely back in the judging ring. I'd do it myself, only I promised Mr. Smith of the AKC that I'd—"

"All right," Gracie agreed at last, feeling cornered. "But he's a grown man. Can't he take care of himself?"

"One would think so." The reply came from over her shoulder.

Gracie spun around. Him! He had heard! She looked up—a long way up. He was a good six foot to her five foot one.

Diane greeted him warmly. "Dr. Phelps! You enjoyed your lunch, I hope. I was just talking with Gracie here, and she has kindly agreed to be your docent for the next hour. I know how confusing these competitions can be to someone who's never attended one before, and you haven't, have you? This is your first?" Without waiting for an answer, she stepped deftly between the good doctor and the judge, who was bearing down upon him again. Collecting his arm and Gracie's, Diane drew them in the opposite direction. "Dr. Stewart handled the last regional competition we had around here," she said, heading for the door. "It was held in Sugar Creek...about five years ago, wasn't it, Gracie?"

Gracie gave a short nod.

Diane continued, blithely ignoring the judge, who was right behind them. "It's a good thing Dr. Stewart chose to work with animals, because he was *terrible* with people." She chuckled. "He had half the breeders avoiding him and the other half searching for a rope and a sturdy tree limb. The man couldn't seem to understand that he was at the competition to deal with any emergencies that might crop up, not to hand out unwanted advice…especially since he didn't hold breeders in very high regard. You would have thought we were all monsters, not animal lovers! You don't agree with that point of view, do you, Dr. Phelps?''

''Dr. Stewart wasn't the world's most tactful person,'' he murmured as they left the dining room and headed toward the lobby.

Gracie noticed that he had deftly avoided answering Diane's question.

The club president laughed. ''That's an understatement if I ever heard one! Now…'' she paused to glance behind them ''…I must excuse myself. Gracie, why don't you and Dr. Phelps…go,'' she finished vaguely, waggling her fingers to speed them on their way. Then she turned to intercept the judge, who was just coming into the hallway. ''Mrs. Wilcox!'' she exclaimed happily. ''Just the person I was looking for! There are so many people who want to meet you! Come with me back into the dining room and I'll…'' Before the accosted woman could do more than squint, she'd been gathered into the determined care of Diane Jennings.

Gracie glanced at Dr. Phelps, then away again. Now what was she going to do? How could she possibly get out of this?

''You don't remember me, do you?'' he prompted.

''Should I?'' she asked, feigning interest in something at the end of the hall.

''I used to bag your groceries at Olsen's Supermarket. At least, I did the one summer I worked there…the summer before you moved away. I had a huge crush on you.''

Gracie's head spun around. He was going back fourteen years! To a time when so much had been happening in her life. Her mother had died the year previously, leaving her for all intents and purposes alone. Gracie had been working at one short-term job after another, all the while trying to find her niche. Then she'd hit on the idea of running a breeding kennel.

''I'm sorry,'' she said levelly, ''I don't remember you.''

His brown eyes took on an even more amused look. ''Nor would I expect you to. Tragically for me, my feelings weren't returned. It didn't seem to matter how carefully I packed your eggs or your bread, all I ever got for my trouble was a polite thank-you.''

''How old were you?'' Gracie asked.

''A man of fourteen.''

''I would have guessed ten,'' she murmured.

''I'd already started to shave.''

People were moving past them on either side. In order not to impede traffic further, Gracie set off down the hall. He fell into step at her side.

''You're Roger Phelps?'' she asked after a moment, for something to say.

''One and the same.''

She frowned. ''Weren't you off in New York studying to be a medical doctor? What are you doing here impersonating a veterinarian?''

"I *am* a veterinarian. I switched fields. I took over Dr. Stewart's practice when he retired."

"I never used Dr. Stewart."

"He was a good vet."

At the lobby she turned to confront him. "I noticed you didn't answer Diane's question earlier. Do you agree with Dr. Stewart? Do you think we're all a bunch of irresponsible breeders willing to destroy our breed in order to win Best of Show? And if you do, why are you here?"

He grimaced. "You don't believe in pulling your punches, do you?"

"It's one of the prerogatives of age."

"How old are you?" he asked, his eyes twinkling.

She was taken aback at his own directness. "Do you enjoy annoying people? Isn't that rather juvenile behavior?" she snapped.

"Not normally. And people usually think I'm very mature for my age."

"Which means you're perfectly capable of taking care of yourself."

"I have been for most of my twenty-eight years."

He was twenty-eight. A little older than she'd originally thought. "Well, Dr. Phelps," she said with deceptive sweetness, "I suggest you continue to do exactly that. You don't need my help!"

She spun on her heels and prepared to stalk away. She wasn't prepared for him to reach out and stop her. Or for the fact that his fingers on her arm set off a reaction that completely unnerved her. She went hot, then cold, then hot again, all in the space of a few seconds.

"Will you have dinner with me tonight?" he asked.

She carefully disengaged her arm. "You must be joking."

"No, for once I'm not."

Gracie looked at him—defiantly at first. Then something happened. The other people in the lobby somehow seemed to fade away. The hustle and bustle, the distant barking of dogs, the rattle of a bellman's cart…it all evaporated, leaving the two of them alone together, suspended in time. She was aware of the tiny pulse at Roger's temple, the masculine curve of his eyebrows, the sensual line of his lips. But beyond his good looks she had a quick intuitive glimpse of the man inside. A man who, though still young, had a confidence in himself that came from a solid core. From strong Midwestern values that she shared.

"…Don't care what you say, Eddie. Letting these—these *animals* run loose is wrong. It's a bad idea! *Bad!*"

The sentiment, uttered in guttural English by an elderly man, burst the bubble that had temporarily surrounded them and brought Gracie back to reality with a hard thump. She hadn't felt like that—evidencing such deep interest in a man—since she and Paul—

"They are destroying the grounds, ruining the hedges!" the old man complained. "Many bushes will die, will have to be replaced. And the noise! Yap, yap, yap. All the time *yap!* This morning I saw a huge one—one of the big ones, you know?—and it had curlers in its hair. Curlers! Now I ask you, is that a proper dog?''

''They aren't going to hurt anything, Dad. Not permanently,'' Edward Wocheck patiently explained.

''It's still a bad idea,'' the man Gracie now recognized as Philip Wocheck continued. ''The gardener will complain. And the guests…someone will get bitten!''

Beside her, Roger Phelps spoke up. ''Mr. Wocheck, these are very well-trained animals. I seriously doubt they'll bite anyone.''

The two men looked at him, and Roger leaned forward and extended his hand. ''Roger Phelps, the show veterinarian,'' he said by way of introduction.

''Phelps?'' Edward echoed.

''George Phelps's son,'' Roger explained. ''My office is in town.''

''Of course,'' Edward said, gripping his hand. ''I remember hearing—''

''They make too much noise!'' his father persisted, determined to be difficult. ''And they make messes on the lawn!''

''Everyone has been instructed to be very careful in that regard,'' Gracie said, speaking up as well. ''Pooper scoopers and waste bags have been provided. I saw to it myself. If you see anyone not following the rules, point them out and I'll have a word with them.'' She smiled and extended her own hand. ''I'm Gracie Lawson.''

She remembered Edward Wocheck, but she doubted if he remembered her. Even though he'd grown up in Tyler, and his father had at one time been the groundskeeper of Timberlake Lodge when it was privately owned by the Ingalls family, he now moved in a high-powered world where the past might easily be forgotten.

"Sheila's aunt!" Edward smiled.

He had identified a connection, but Gracie doubted he remembered her. But then, why should he? Almost as many years separated them as separated herself and Roger Phelps.

Gracie glanced to the side and saw that Roger was watching her, and that his eyes were once again twinkling. He didn't wink again—she would have died if he had—but that same bold awareness, that appreciation of her as a woman, filled his gaze.

"They are not proper dogs," Phil grumbled. "A Great Dane...now *that* is a dog! Or a Mastiff! You would never see one of them wearing *curlers!*" He spat the last word as he started to move away.

"My father is set in his ways, but he's not always this disagreeable," Edward said in a low tone. "I'm certain he'd be very sorry if he thought he'd offended you." Then he caught up with the older man and gently led him down the hall.

"Have there been other complaints?" Roger Phelps asked.

"Only one that I know of," Gracie replied.

"You do this a lot? Hold dog shows in hotels?"

"This isn't the first. Now, if you'll excuse me..." She wanted to get away from him before whatever it was that had happened between them occurred again. She still felt thrown off balance by her feelings, by her thoughts.

"What about tonight?" he persisted. "Dinner?" he explained when she looked at him blankly.

She shook her head. "I don't think so."

"Why not?"

He had a gorgeous smile, she'd give him that. And a nice face, open and fun-loving. What would it hurt to go out with him? To remember a bit of the sizzle and breathlessness brought on by an attentive male?

"I can't," she said. "I'm having dinner with friends tonight."

"Tomorrow night, then," he said quickly.

"No... I don't—it's not..."

"For old times' sake," he urged her. "To fulfill a bag boy's dreams."

She couldn't help it; she smiled. But she had to put an end to this! "Look!" she said firmly, trying to sound sensible and reasonable. "This isn't going to happen, all right? I don't know what kind of game you're playing, or if... Has someone put you up to this? Was it Sheilie?"

As soon as the thought occurred to her she looked around for her niece. Was this one of Sheila's little tricks? She was always dropping hints, letting Gracie know that she thought it was time for her to start looking for another mate. Since Sheila's marriage to Douglas in August, the hints had gotten stronger.

"A game?" Roger Phelps echoed blankly.

Gracie turned back to him. If Sheilie was watching them, she was doing so from a well-hidden spot.

"Just leave me alone, all right? I don't want to play. I don't have time for... Just leave me alone!"

To emphasize her point Gracie stamped her foot,

only to feel totally discomforted when his gaze, which had dropped in amusement to the floor, made a slow, appreciative returning sweep over her body, not missing a thing.

"All right," he agreed softly. "I'll leave you alone."

But that wasn't the message in his warm golden brown eyes. His eyes were promising much more to come.

Present-day convention called for Gracie to confront him, to lecture him about the folly of unwanted sexual harassment. But how could she do that when every nerve ending in her body was aflame?

BY THE TIME Gracie collected herself, Sheila had breezed through the door from the hotel offices to speak to the desk clerk. Gracie headed straight for her.

"Sheilie," she said briskly, "I want a word with you."

Sheila's hazel eyes widened.

"In private," Gracie continued, her voice clipped.

Her niece immediately took them to a quiet corner. "What is it?" she asked, concerned. "Has something happened to one of the guests? Has one of the dogs—"

Gracie interrupted her. "The joke's gone as far as it's going to, Sheilie. I'm not going to play, and I don't appreciate the fact that you think I'd enjoy—"

"What joke?" Sheila asked, frowning.

"You can call your boy off now."

"What boy? I don't know what you're talking about."

The denial was made with such genuine puzzlement that Gracie was momentarily rattled. "Dr. Phelps," she explained, regaining her former ire.

Sheila shook her head. "Aunt Grace, I don't know what you're talking about. Dr. Phelps? Dr. George Phelps? What has he—"

"Not George! *Roger!*"

"You've been working too hard. You're under too much stress. Selling the kennel, moving back into Tyler...those things were very hard on you emotionally."

"The only thing I am 'emotionally' is angry! I don't need you to find a man for me, Sheilie! Especially one barely out of diapers!"

Her niece continued to stare at her. Then something clicked and her frown turned into a dawning smile. "Is Roger Phelps coming on to you? Oh my goodness! Isn't that a treat! Roger Phelps...he's quite a catch!"

"If you put him up to this, Sheilie—"

"I didn't! I swear!" Sheila grinned. "What did he do? What did he say? Tell me everything!"

Gracie was in more of an unnerved state now than she had been moments before. Sheilie hadn't had a hand in it? Then that meant... "Don't lie to me, Sheilie!" she warned.

"I'm not lying! Cross my heart and hope to die!" Her niece made the appropriate motions.

"Oh...my...God." Gracie breathed. The air around her suddenly seemed too thin. She needed to sit down. She looked for a chair. Because if what Sheila said was true—and it was—that meant Roger Phelps's at-

tentions had been for real. He had responded to her on his own, without prompting. Which meant that he—

"Over here!" Her niece saw her into a wingback chair half-hidden from view by a tall palm. It was positioned close to a glass-paneled door leading outside. "Do you need a glass of water? Something stronger?"

While Sheila's words evidenced concern, there was an amused lilt in her voice. Gracie declined.

"You look so shocked!" Sheila chided. "You're a very attractive woman, Aunt Grace. That's what I keep telling you! It's wrong for you to be so solitary. Just because you had a bad experience doesn't mean—"

Gracie cut her off. "He's a baby!" she exclaimed.

"Roger Phelps? He's almost as old as I am. Twenty-eight or twenty-nine, I should think."

"He's twenty-eight. He told me."

Sheila's smile increased. "So we're already into intimate details!"

Gracie stood up. "A person's age isn't an intimate detail!"

"Has he asked you to go out with him? What did you say?"

"I turned him down, of course."

"Why 'of course'? Why didn't you accept?" Sheila was right behind her as she walked away. "Because you thought I'd put him up to it? Aunt Grace! I didn't. I swear I didn't!"

"I believe you," Gracie said tightly.

"Then what are you going to do?" They'd stopped just short of the front desk.

"Nothing," Gracie replied.

Her niece frowned. "Aunt Grace—"

"Absolutely nothing! And I'd appreciate it if you would kindly respect that decision."

"May I hope?" Sheila countered impudently.

Gracie sent her a pointed look. "Instead of worrying about me so much, you might be better off seeing to your livelihood. Phil Wocheck is highly displeased about the dog show. I did the best I could, but when he left he was still grumbling…to Edward."

"But Mr. Wocheck—Edward—okayed the dog show personally! I always give him a complete report on each group we're planning to host, and he signs off on it before the final scheduling. This time, because it involved animals, I made a specific point of double-checking with him, just to be on the safe side."

"It seems no one checked with his father."

Sheila grimaced. "Offering an upgrade isn't going to work in this instance, is it?"

"Not when he already has a perfectly nice suite in the family quarters."

"I'd better talk with Edward."

"At least he defended the dog show to his father."

"That's something," Sheila said. She started to walk away, then turned back to whisper, "If he asks again, say yes!"

Gracie pretended ignorance. *"Edward Wocheck?"*

"No," Sheila said dryly. "Not Edward Wocheck. You know who I mean."

"Playing in a nursery is not my idea of a good time."

Sheila's eyes narrowed. "Just what *is*, Aunt Grace?" She arched an eyebrow and walked briskly away.

CHAPTER THREE

IT WAS A NUMBER OF hectic hours later when Gracie let herself into the small house she rented in Tyler. Though barely more than a cottage, it served her purposes nicely. With only herself and the two small dogs to care for, she didn't need a lot of space.

Jacques and Jo-Jo greeted her at the door. Jo-Jo bounced and yipped and wagged his short tail rapidly, while Jacques, as befitted a much older dog, merely wagged his tail.

"Hello, boys," she said. She made her way to the couch and sat down so that they could greet her properly. Both were excited that she was home. "Did you miss me?" she asked, rubbing their curly black hair.

"Yarp!" Jo-Jo replied, before taking a flying leap off the couch. *"Yarp!"*

"Outside, then food…right?" she asked him. He started to run, his toenails digging into the rug. "You, too?" She looked at Jacques. His front paws danced on the arm cushion.

To save his fourteen-year-old legs, Gracie lifted him down to the rug. Jacques had been her first dog when she'd started the breeding kennel. She'd raised him from a pup. It had taken her several years and a number of other carefully made acquisitions to actually get the program going, but Jacques had always held place of honor in her heart. Even if he hadn't gone on to be a repeat champion—which he had—she would have loved him.

"All right, then, let's go." She put their harnesses on and attached their leads. Jo-Jo was first out the door.

The house had a nice little backyard, but the dogs missed the long tramps she used to take them on at the farm. She believed in exercising a dog naturally to keep it in shape. The outings were also good for her. While she walked—strolled, actually, as the dogs moved from one interesting scent to another—she could let her mind wander. She didn't question her sanity for giving up the successful business she'd spent years nurturing, or for leaving the comfortable home she'd made in the country, but tonight let her thoughts dwell on other things. The beautiful fall foliage, the sharp nip in the air, the scent of burning firewood…laughing golden-brown eyes.

Gracie brought her musings to an abrupt halt. She was *not* going to think about Roger Phelps. Just as she wasn't going to let herself think about Paul. The day had been far too much of a strain, with her pretending that everything was fine in her life and going the way she wanted, when in fact nothing was fine and she had no idea of what she truly wanted. She was at a crossroads. She'd made two of the bigger decisions of her life in the last few months—she'd sold the kennel and she'd moved into Tyler, temporarily at least. Her lease was for a year. But after that? After that she didn't have the slightest idea. Grace

Farms was out of her hands now. The money was in the bank—more money than she'd ever expected to possess. She could do as she pleased for a time. Whatever that might be.

Gracie thought of the dinner she'd just shared with Raymond and Claudette. When they'd finally met at the show she had sensed their curiosity. Probing looks had been followed by the invitation to dinner, and Gracie had agreed, precisely because she didn't want to. The couple presented the largest hurdle she had to get over during these two days, and she didn't want them carrying stories back to certain interested parties that she was still suffering. So she had met them and laughed and talked, catching up on old times. They told her Paul and Jessica were parents now, of a baby boy. Gracie hadn't flinched. She'd even asked them to take back her good wishes....

Jacques pulled on his lead, trying to stray off the sidewalk into a yard. She brought him back with a quiet admonishment.

Someone who knew her history might question her decision to help coordinate the dog show, considering how difficult she'd known it was going to be. But it was something she had to do before she could start her new life. Gracie also saw it as a small repayment to Diane Jennings. The club president was one of the people who'd stuck up for her, as Barbara had, against Paul. And when Diane came back to the Tyler area she hadn't breathed a word to anyone, saving Gracie from further humiliation at the hands of the local gossips.

Gracie called to the dogs to turn back, and as she

did, she laughed wryly to herself. She wasn't very good at not thinking about things, was she?

ROGER PHELPS CLIMBED the stairs leading to his rooms above the veterinary clinic. He'd just come from checking the condition of his overnight patients, two cats and a dog. One of the cats had gotten into something caustic, irritating his eyes and breathing passage. The other feline had an injured leg, and the dog was a stray someone had dropped off the day before.

Serra waited patiently on the landing, as she had since becoming a member of his household the previous January.

Once, she'd undoubtedly been a beautiful specimen of a golden retriever. The day she'd been brought to him—carried in by a dairy farmer who lived on the outskirts of town—she'd been left for dead in a ditch, almost frozen, with numerous broken bones and extensive internal injuries caused by repeated blows and kicks. To top it all off, she'd been in danger of losing vision in one eye and had twitched when anyone so much as spoke to her.

At first Roger had debated euthanasia. He wasn't sure if it would be more of a kindness to release her from her misery or try to nurse her back to health. But something within Serra had stayed his hand and encouraged him to work to reclaim her. Despite the mistreatment she'd endured, despite her fear, she'd licked his wrist while he'd examined her. One weak touch of tongue to skin, one hopeful look from her good eye and she'd stolen his heart.

He didn't leave her side for the next twenty-four hours, and later, when other veterinary duties demanded his attention, he came back to her as often as possible.

It had been a long, hard struggle, but they'd managed it. Emotionally, though, Serra trusted no one but him. Which had made it difficult when he went through the motions of trying to find her a good home. By the end of May he'd had to stop kidding himself. He had found a dog that was his.

Serra brushed her feathery tail against the hardwood floor and came to greet him. She accepted his greeting shyly, her tail increasing its sweep.

Her coat had grown back almost like new; her injuries had healed, as had her eye. She still moved slowly, though, and limped, seemingly old before her time. To the best of Roger's knowledge, she was probably six or seven. She'd had several litters of pups by the time she'd come to him, but was unable to bear more. He'd have spayed her anyway, on general principle, but her injuries had necessitated it. She'd also had a number of previously broken bones.

"How's my sweetheart?" he asked warmly as he stroked her head.

She leaned against him, her most obvious show of affection.

"Are you hungry, girl?" he asked. "Did Fiona feed you?"

Fiona Evans was his office assistant. She answered the phones, made appointments and assisted him in surgery.

Serra followed him into the kitchen. Her food bowl

was still partially full. She didn't eat quickly. She savored her meals, making them last—an odd idiosyncrasy for a dog who one might expect would gobble everything quickly in case it disappeared.

"Ah, so she did," Roger said.

Serra 'let' Fiona care for her when Roger was away. She waited under the kitchen table and watched as her bowls were filled with food and fresh water. And if she needed a trip outside into the backyard, she trailed several paces behind. She never let Fiona touch her, always ducking aside as if she expected to be hit.

Fiona, who'd loved animals all her life, had been hurt at first. She had wanted to shower the abused animal with affection. But Serra knew her own mind, and Fiona had come to respect her ways.

Roger set about preparing his own meal, a quick stir-fry in a wok. He wasn't particularly hungry, but he knew he had to eat something. Jacob Beamish had a pregnant cow that had given them trouble the last two times she'd given birth. Roger had to be prepared for a call at any time.

He heated some cooked rice in his microwave and covered it with the contents of the wok—tender strips of chicken, snow peas, thinly cut carrots and green onions seasoned with soy sauce and curry. The aroma was wonderful and his appetite quickened.

His cooking wasn't of the same caliber as the chef at Timberlake Lodge, but it held body and spirit together. Serra obviously thought so, too, silently resting her chin on his knee after he sat down at the table.

When he slipped her a small strip of chicken, she ate it with relish.

Timberlake Lodge... Roger stabbed a snow pea with his fork and chewed it consideringly. What an interesting day he'd had. Seen what a dog show was like up close, met any number of friendly breeders, found the woman he wanted to marry....

He laughed out loud, startling Serra. To pacify her, he fondled her ear.

Gracie Lawson. He'd noticed her first thing that morning. She hadn't seen him. She'd been too busy, bustling here and there, dealing with one problem after another, taking her job as liaison very seriously. But she'd done it all in a friendly manner, charming everyone with her smile.

He wasn't kidding when he'd told her that he'd once been her bag boy, or that he'd had a huge crush on her. To his fourteen-year-old eyes she was the most attractive woman he'd ever seen, and the age difference between them simply added spice. Only the start of football practice had dragged him out of his depression when she'd moved away from town and never come back. At least, she never returned to Olsen's Supermarket, not in the short time he'd continued to work there the remainder of that summer. She might have moved to the Arctic, as far as he was concerned.

Roger's mother had flatly refused to let him work again at the supermarket the next summer, and his father had gone along with her edict—for a very different reason. His mother didn't think it looked right for the son of one of the town's most prominent families to work alongside the sons of lesser beings. His father had wanted him to spend the summer studying. Roger was about to enter the tenth grade, and he had to get serious about preparing for medical school. His already excellent grades were no longer enough. They had to be better!

In the haze of surging hormones that had made up his teenage years the memories of his first love had faded. Then had come the rigors of medical school, of getting out of medical school and finally of announcing his true intention—to become a veterinarian.

Everything was finally starting to settle down. He had finished his training and taken over Dr. Stewart's practice. Clients all over the Tyler vicinity had come to trust him. Then he'd stumbled into an agreement to be the house veterinarian at the dog show—and because of it, his life would never be the same.

Gracie Lawson. She was just as attractive today as she had been fourteen years ago. Only now he understood why his body had gone into overdrive the instant he'd caught sight of her. She was tiny in stature, yet with a shape that... Hourglass, wasn't that the term? Unfashionable in today's world, where most models closely resembled a stick.

She was feisty and outspoken, yet had a certain vulnerability that made him want to charge into battle on her behalf. And with her feathery blond hair, dark brown eyes, small straight nose and lips that moved easily into a smile, it was all he could do not to kiss her!

Roger smiled as he remembered the way she'd

looked when she'd noticed him for the first time, across the judging ring. And the way she'd adamantly refused to go out with him. She seemed to think he was a boy playing a game.

One thing he wasn't, though, was a boy. And this was definitely not a game.

GRACIE PARKED her car—a little red Miata—in front of the lodge and hurried inside. Before two minutes had passed, she was swallowed up by Sunday's show activities. She didn't get a break until midday, and that was a quick, but necessary, trip home.

"You're leaving?" Sheila asked, happening upon her just outside the main entrance. "I didn't think the show was over until four."

"My next-door neighbor can't give the boys their midday outing. Something to do with a command appearance by her in-laws—that's what she called it."

"That's too bad," Sheila sympathized.

"At least the trip is short. I won't be gone long."

A limousine rolled to a stop before the wide double doors of the hotel's entrance. The driver got out, came around to the passenger door in back and, instead of opening it, immediately started to rub at an offending spot of dirt.

"Someone important is leaving?" Gracie asked.

"Lady Holmes. This was just a quick stopover on her way to London." Sheila paused. "Oh, that reminds me. I spoke with Glenna last night. She said her parents still haven't heard anything from Kathleen."

"Poor things." Gracie frowned. "What in the world was Kathleen thinking?"

"Glenna doesn't know. Her only clue is something Kathleen wrote in a letter once—something about making a new friend from that part of the world. Maybe that has something to do with it."

Gracie shrugged. The Adriatic country was a long way from Tyler.

Sheila leaned closer. "I also learned something else. Not about Kathleen, but about Mr. Wocheck...both Mr. Wochecks. Edward is worried about his father. Old Phil has been acting a lot like Dad did right after Mom died—he's unusually quiet and has to be persuaded to leave his room. In some ways, the dog show has probably been good for him. It's riled him up. If Edward's like we were, seeing his dad act grumpy is better than nothing at all." She paused for a moment, considering. "I wonder if we should say anything...because of what we went through with Dad."

"Did Edward Wocheck tell you this personally?" Gracie asked.

"No."

"Then it might not be a good thing. He might not like the idea that people are talking behind their backs."

"He knows Tyler."

"Still..."

Sheila sighed. "You're probably right. I'll bide my time and only say something if the moment presents itself." Her attention was caught by activity in the parking lot. A smile suddenly brightened her features. "Look who's coming," she said softly.

Gracie glanced around, narrowed her eyes and saw the object of Sheila's attention. Roger Phelps! So far that morning she'd managed to avoid him. And she really wanted to keep it that way. Overnight, she'd decided that she'd blown yesterday all out of proportion because of the tension she'd been under. But she didn't want to put that theory to a test. Not yet, at any rate!

Her first instinct was to find cover. She tried to push Sheilie back into the lobby, where they'd be less noticeable, but her niece wouldn't budge.

"Roger! Hello!" Sheila called to him, insuring that he'd see them.

Gracie sent her an irritated look, then did her best to don an expression of unconcern.

"Sheila," he said, coming up to them. "Gracie." He included her in his smile.

Gracie could feel his amused scrutiny. Had he seen her attempt to get away? She gave him a tight nod.

Sheila was grinning like a Cheshire cat. "It's just amazing, isn't it?" she said brightly. "All these poodles! Have you ever seen so many in one place before?"

"Never."

"I see you've met my aunt Gracie. But did you know she's a very talented breeder of toy poodles herself?"

"*Was,* Sheilie," Gracie murmured. "I'm not anymore. I've retired."

Sheila laughed. "That makes you sound like you're

ready to shuffle off to Worthington House! Don't be silly!''

Gracie had to restrain herself from giving her niece a shake.

"I heard a number of good things about Grace Farms yesterday," Roger said. "Your fellow breeders all agree that it's a first-class operation."

Gracie looked at him. What else had he heard? "It's out of my hands now," she said gruffly.

"I heard that, too. Why?"

Gracie pretended to miss the meddlesome question. She glanced at her watch and made a face. "I'm sorry, Sheilie, but I have to leave. If I don't, I won't get home and back before the next round of judging begins." She tried to look nonchalant as she broke away, as if it wasn't an escape.

Roger Phelps quickly caught up to her. "Have you been avoiding me?" he asked quietly, falling into step at her side.

"I don't know what you mean," Gracie replied.

"Every time I come near you, you flit away."

"I haven't seen you."

He slanted her a smile. "You haven't?"

She flashed him an annoyed look. "Do you think I spend my day watching out for you?"

"That would be nice," he replied softly.

"Then you're not just an optimist, you're a dreamer."

He stopped her forward progress by stepping in front of her. "Do you know what it does to me when you look at me like that?"

Gracie unwillingly met his gaze. "I wouldn't hazard a guess,'' she said and slipped around him. She walked fast, hoping that he wouldn't follow. She was finding it harder and harder to continue brushing him off. But again he caught up with her.

By that time, though, she was at her car. All she wanted was to hop in and drive away, leaving him to do whatever it was he wanted that didn't involve her. Only, to her dismay, she saw that the driver's-side front tire was completely flat.

He followed her gaze. ''Is this yours?'' he asked.

''Oh, great! Just great!'' she exclaimed, clutching her shoulder bag. On the way to the lodge that morning she'd been forced to run through some road debris. It was either that or make a dangerous, last-minute swerve. She'd worried at the time that trouble could result, but when nothing had happened immediately, she'd thought she was safe.

He went to the front of the car and squatted down. ''Here's the problem,'' he said, running his fingers over the rubber tread. ''It's metal and it's sharp.'' He stood up. ''It must be long, too, to imbed itself like that.''

Gracie looked from the flat tire to the lodge entrance. Several options were open to her, none of them appealing. She could pull a dog-show friend away from lunch and ask to be run home and back, she could find out if Sheila had her car that day and ask to borrow it, or she could call the garage in town and wait for Carl to get here, putting her far behind schedule.

''Here, hold this,'' Roger Phelps instructed, pushing his jacket at her.

Gracie frowned. "Why? What are you—"

"I'm going to change your tire."

When she still wouldn't take it, he laid it on the Miata's hood and started to roll up his sleeves. "Is your spare in the trunk?" he asked.

"I can't ask you to do this. It's not—"

"Do you even know where your spare is?"

Gracie blinked. He was smiling at her, amused. She pointed wordlessly toward the back.

"I'll need your keys," he said.

She reached inside her purse. She didn't want him to have to do it, but she didn't want to disturb other people, either, or be late.

He worked quickly and efficiently, and within ten minutes her little car was no longer listing as badly.

"Tell you what," he said, wiping his hands on a paper towel he'd found in her trunk. "Why don't I take you home, and on the way we'll drop the flat off at Carl's Garage? He'll fix it and get someone up here to change it for you when he's done. It shouldn't take long. Then you'll be all ready to go when the show's over, like it never happened."

Gracie had difficulty getting past his first sentence. "I can drive myself home," she said. "That's what a spare is for."

"Not one of these undersize things. They aren't meant to be used except in emergencies."

"This isn't an emergency?" she countered, looking up at him.

"Not in my book," he said, grinning.

It definitely was in Gracie's. He was just as appealing today as he had been yesterday, and just as determined. But as she looked at the puny excuse for a spare tire, she reluctantly nodded. "All right," she said. "But I want to pay you for the gas…and for changing the tire."

"The tire's on me," he said. "And the gas? We're only going to Tyler, aren't we?"

"Yes, but I'll definitely pay for the gas. That's my condition."

He shook his head as he reclaimed his jacket from the hood and said drolly, "I promise I'll tell you to the last milliliter."

"Thank you," she said. Then, belatedly, she thanked him for changing the tire as well.

He took her to a late-model van that had the logo of his veterinary clinic painted on each front door. Animal Crackers had been the name chosen by old Dr. Stewart when he'd first come to Tyler, and Roger Phelps had kept it.

As Gracie settled into the passenger seat her eyes widened at the van's contents. This was a nearly complete pet hospital on wheels! It had an X-ray machine, a well-appointed lab and supply base, a cleverly adapted examination area.

"How do you like it?" he asked, starting the engine.

"It's wonderful!" she exclaimed. "You have everything in here!"

"Almost everything. It's my pride and joy. If my patients were limited to Tyler, I wouldn't need it. But a good portion of them are on farms."

"Dr. Stewart didn't have anything like this, did he?"

Roger reversed out of the parking slot. "No, it's my contribution to the practice. Sometimes I'd feel so hamstrung when I was out on a call, wishing I had something from back at the clinic. So I decided to bring as much of it with me as I could."

"It's a great idea!"

He smiled. "I'm glad I've finally done something that meets with your approval."

Gracie twisted forward in her seat and thought about things as Roger drove down the long, curving lane toward the lakeshore road. Was she being unfair to him? Judging him harshly because of his relative youth and the way he looked? It was obvious that he was well thought of, and not just because he came from a prominent old Tyler family. If he wanted to amuse himself by having a light flirtation with an older woman, who was she to say that it was wrong? Older men did that with younger women all the time…something she knew about firsthand. And not just only light flirtations; sometimes they got married and had babies.…

She folded her hands on her lap and, pushing away her unwanted thoughts of Paul and Jessica, looked at him. "I've always believed that a good veterinarian is a necessity of life," she said sweetly. And when he frowned slightly, confused by her sudden capitulation, her smile grew wider.

THEY DROPPED THE TIRE off at Carl's Garage, with his assurance that her little sports car would be back in service by the end of the afternoon.

"It'll be done by four," Carl promised. "Can't see

where there should be any problem. Davey here will run her up to the lodge for you the minute it's ready.'' He indicated his assistant, who was at that moment stretched out over a truck engine.

"Thanks, Carl," Gracie said.

Carl looked from Gracie to Roger and back again. "Not a problem," he said easily, but Gracie could read curiosity in his gaze. Had he picked up on some of the fine tension snapping in the air between them?

She climbed back into the van and waited for Roger to restart the engine.

"Where to?" he asked.

"Morgan and Fifth."

The engine purred to life and the van rolled away.

"How long do you need?" Roger asked.

"Fifteen minutes. But I can cut it shorter."

"No need. I thought I might stop by the clinic. My assistant paged me earlier with a question about one of our patients. She's perfectly capable of handling it on her own, but since I'm in town…"

Gracie glanced at the cellular telephone mounted between the seats. "Is that what you were doing in the lodge parking lot? Using that to talk to her?"

He nodded. "I prefer it to a pay phone. Far less noise and distraction.

"Jacques and Jo-Jo will be happy with any time they get."

"Your famous poodles." He smiled, causing her to wonder yet again what all he'd heard about her. "You'll have to introduce me sometime," he said.

They drew up to the front of her house, and Gracie hopped out. She started to close the door, then thought better of it. Her conscience was still pricking for her earlier grumpiness. He had helped her, after all. Gone far out of his way to be of assistance. "Listen," she began, "I really appreciate what you've—"

She got no further. The telephone signaled a call and Roger answered it. Then, frowning, he asked a couple of questions. After hanging up, he looked at her. "Would it be a problem if we cut your stop to five minutes? Jacob Beamish has a cow in trouble. I'll wait here while you take your dogs out, then drop you back at the lodge."

Gracie gazed at him earnestly. "I can borrow a neighbor's car or something. You don't have to take me back to the lodge."

"It's on my way. And if you borrow a car, you'd have to deal with getting it back later."

"Jacob Beamish's cow?" Gracie murmured.

"Every year she has trouble calving. I promised I'd drop everything when he called—even the dog show. My assistant is arranging for someone to take my place at the lodge. I don't know how long I'll be."

Gracie realized that she was delaying him. She quickly closed the door, hurried to her house, greeted the boys and let them out into the backyard. As she waited for them to make use of their short-term freedom, she thought about the change that had come over Roger Phelps the instant he'd received the call. Whereas before he'd been teasing and lighthearted, a call to duty had turned him completely serious. It was apparent that he cared deeply about the animals in his charge and was there for them when they needed him.

Gracie found that attribute more appealing than his good looks.

After calling the boys inside and checking their bowls, she hurried back to the van.

CHAPTER FOUR

GRACIE MADE HER WAY tiredly to the parking lot a little after five, expecting to find her Miata all repaired and waiting. It wasn't. It continued to list toward the driver's-side front, the undersized spare still in place.

For a moment all she could do was stare at it. Carl hadn't done as he'd promised! Neither he nor his assistant had come to Timberlake Lodge to make the necessary switch! She checked her watch, even though the growing gloom signaled the approach of evening. Then she took what she knew would be a futile look around. No Carl. No Davey.

A short time later Sheila found her sitting in the car with the door open. "Aunt Grace?" she ventured, coming closer.

"Sheilie, hello!" Gracie responded wryly. "I was just debating whether to boil Carl in oil or merely tar and feather him!"

Sheila glanced at the undersize tire. After being delivered back to the hotel at midday, Gracie had told her what had happened. "Wasn't he supposed to change that?"

"He was."

Sheila frowned. "I wonder why he didn't. He's usually so reliable."

Gracie swung her feet into the car. "I'm going to take it home. If I drive slowly, everything should be just fine."

"I can take you home," Sheila offered quickly.

Gracie threw her a skeptical look. "Aren't you supposed to be meeting Douglas in Sugar Creek for dinner and a movie in half an hour?"

"Yes, but I can call and tell him I'm going to be late."

"I'd rather not leave my car sitting here all night," Gracie said.

"It would be perfectly safe."

A large vehicle rolled to a stop behind them. Both women looked around, expecting Carl, but for some reason Gracie wasn't surprised to see that it was Roger Phelps instead, in his van.

"He didn't come?" Roger asked, just as surprised as they were.

"I'm trying to convince her to let me take her home," Sheila said, "but she's worried about the car."

Roger reached for his cell phone. After dialing a number, he listened for a long time before hanging up. "No one's at the garage," he said. "It must be closed."

Sheila shook her head. "This just isn't like Carl."

"Maybe an emergency repair came up, causing him to run late." Roger looked at Gracie. "I'm on my way into Tyler. Why don't you let me drop you off? Then when Carl finally does arrive and looks for the car, he'll find it, fix it and I'll bet he'll bring it home to you…with an apology. What do you think?"

"I think this is fast becoming a farce," Gracie grumbled.

"Roger's right," Sheila agreed. "If you take it home, Carl won't know where to find you. He doesn't know where you live now, does he?"

"No."

The lights in the parking lot switched on, causing a pale golden glow to illuminate the area.

Gracie didn't want to get into the van with Roger again. She was so exhausted from the last two days— a particularly busy time helping to run the show. But with the added stress of constantly maintaining a face-saving front, she was almost at the end of her rope. Her nerves were on edge, her defenses were severely depleted. She fought a short battle in her mind, then admitted defeat. "All right," she said tiredly. "If Dr. Phelps wants to—"

"Roger," he interjected.

"—Take me home, he can."

"I didn't bite earlier, did I?" he chided humorously.

Sheila laughed, then did her best to hide it when Gracie sent her a jaundiced look.

Gracie stepped out of the Miata, locked it and walked around the front of the van to the passenger door. This was the last thing she had expected to be doing this evening. Darn Carl! Darn Davey! Darn whoever had dropped the debris on the road!

She settled in the front seat and waved at Sheila as they drew away.

For a time afterward she said nothing, then finally

she asked, "Why did you come back to the lodge? How could you possibly know that Carl—"

"I didn't know," Roger said.

"Then how—"

"I was passing by on my way from Jacob Beamish's farm, and thought I'd check."

"Johnny-on-the-Spot!"

"Roger," he corrected.

"I'm going to have a word with Carl," she said irritably. "What if I'd have had plans tonight? What if—"

"Do you?" he interrupted.

"Do I what?"

"Have plans."

"No, but if…" Too late she saw the trap she'd set for herself. She amended, "Nothing, that is, except a long soak and to go to bed early. I'm very tired."

Roger laughed. "So am I. I wasn't going to ask you out again. Not tonight, at any rate."

Gracie remembered the trouble that had called him out to Jacob Beamish's dairy farm. "How's the cow doing?" she asked. "Did she have the baby?"

"A beautiful little heifer. The mom's doing fine, too. It took a bit—things were touch and go for a while—but the job was well done in the end."

"I love babies," Gracie murmured, letting her head fall back against the headrest. "It doesn't matter what kind. They're all adorable. Baby chicks, baby horses, baby cats and dogs…"

"Especially poodles."

"Yes."

"Which dog won Best of Show?" he asked.

"Are you really interested?"

Roger sent her a sideways look. "I was at the hotel for most of the two days and watched as many competitions as I could."

"Do you remember a black Standard named Buddy? That's what he answers to, of course. On his registration papers he's known as King's Ebony Knight III."

"I remember him. He's a real beauty."

"He won."

"What happens next?" Roger asked. "Does he move on to another level?"

"He goes to another show, then another and another...the goal being to win Best in Show at an all-breed show. Eventually, he could be among the top dogs in his breed."

"And what will that get him?" Roger asked.

Gracie smiled. "Fame and a full stud program."

"A champion's puppies are worth a lot of money, aren't they?"

"They are," she agreed.

"So how does that benefit the dog?"

"He has a good life. He gets to sire a number of offspring. He continues competing. You must have seen the way the dogs enjoy the competition. They can feel the enthusiasm of the crowd—they love the applause. They know when they look good. They know when they've been singled out as a finalist. They know when they've won!"

"You make them sound like athletes or beauty contestants."

"Because they are! Both! That's it exactly. They're

the cream of the crop—among the best of their breed.''

''And what about the ones that aren't?'' he asked quietly.

Gracie's fingers curled. So they were back to that. ''Who aren't…what?'' she asked carefully.

''The best. The ones who are the mistakes. The genetic time bombs waiting to go off.''

''No responsible breeder would ever purpose-fully—''

''Are all breeders responsible?'' He glanced away from the road to add quickly, ''Not that I'm saying you aren't responsible. Or that any of the breeders I've met over the last couple of days aren't, either. I just—''

Adrenalin absorbed some of her tiredness. ''You agree with Dr. Stewart! We're all terrible people who are hell bent on hurting the animals we profess to love, just for the sake of money and prestige.''

''I didn't say that,'' he insisted.

''It sounded like it to me!''

They were fast approaching her house. Gracie reached for the door handle. She'd known it was a mistake to catch a lift with Roger in the first place.

The van halted and Gracie hopped out. ''Thanks for the ride,'' she said shortly. She didn't expect him to come with her, but he was right behind her as she walked stiffly up the pathway to the front porch.

''Gracie,'' he said. ''I didn't mean to insult you.''

She searched the depths of her shoulder bag for her house key. He stood next to her, and to avoid him, she turned away. Lipstick, compact, tiny package of

Kleenex, loose change…where were the keys? She'd returned them to her purse earlier. She knew she had!

He touched her arm. "Gracie," he said again.

She found them! She pulled them free and aimed the proper one at the keyhole.

His hand slid down her jacket to the bare skin of her wrist.

Shock stayed all motion. She might have been turned to stone. Only stone had no feeling, the exact opposite of the tumult that was suddenly taking place within her. She could barely breathe.

His fingers ran smoothly, lightly over the back of her hand.

She looked up at him…and once again the rest of the world dissolved. In the half light provided by the street lamp Gracie saw only his face and the growing hunger in his eyes.

Warm skin on warm skin, a touch as faint and delicate as a butterfly's wing—his lips brushed her cheek on their way to her lips.

What took place next was the sweetest, most shattering kiss that Gracie had ever received. Not even Paul had kissed her like that, setting everything within her instantly on fire.

"Good night, lovely Grace," Roger murmured softly, once he'd pulled away. "Sleep tight."

Tiny toenails tapped against the door. A set of questioning barks followed. As Roger walked back to his van, Gracie turned slowly in a daze to answer the summons. "I'm here, boys. It's me," she said.

Somehow she managed to finish unlocking the door. Before opening it, though, she spared another quick glance at the van, only to see it disappearing down Morgan Avenue.

Had the kiss really happened? she asked herself. Or, in her exhaustion, had she merely imagined it? Instinctively, she lifted a finger to her still-tingling lips. Yes, it definitely had happened.

AN HOUR LATER another car pulled into Gracie's driveway. It was her little red Miata, with Carl himself behind the wheel.

"I can't tell you how sorry I am about this," he said when he came to the door. "Davey had an accident and got cut real bad. I had to run him to the emergency room and wait until he got sewed up. He didn't want to go home, but I made him—drove him there myself. It put us way behind, with only me to do the work. Did you have any trouble getting home?"

Gracie looked at him. *Trouble?* Her answer would depend upon his meaning of the word. If he meant had she had a hard time getting home, the answer was no. But trouble had definitely happened along the way!

"No, no trouble," she said lightly, which brought a relieved smile to his face.

Gracie reached for her purse. But when she opened it, he stopped her. "I'm not going to charge you for this," he said. "It wouldn't be fair."

Gracie handed him the agreed-upon amount. "It wouldn't be fair not to pay you," she said quietly. "None of this was your fault."

Carl slipped the bills into the front pocket of his

work shirt, raised his finger to the oil-smeared brim of his baseball cap, then hurried to the car that waited for him on the opposite side of the street.

Trouble. Gracie again considered the word as she secured the door for the night. Davey had had trouble, so Carl had had trouble…and so, on down the line, had she. One circumstance leading to another, almost as if it had been planned, in a cosmic sense, that Roger Phelps would bring her home that evening. And that before he left, they would kiss…. Had all these events been set in motion yesterday morning when she'd looked up to catch him watching her from across the show ring?

Gracie shook her head. No. This was her tiredness talking. All her defenses were down, letting in silly, meaningless thoughts.

Debris on the roadway, the resulting flat tire, Davey's accident. Roger's appearance at just the right time… Circles, rings extending outward.

Gracie shook her head again.

She didn't believe in fate. She didn't believe that occurrences were already written and just waiting for you to stumble onto them. What she believed in was good old-fashioned determination. And she was very determined that this was where the whole fiasco was going to end!

ROGER'S ASSISTANT, Fiona Evans, was still at the clinic when he returned. She looked up from her place at the reception desk, her round face breaking into its usual smile.

Fiona had the sunniest disposition Roger had ever

seen. She rarely seemed to have a bad day, or even a bad few minutes. Her husband, Wade, in his mid-forties like her, was a long-haul truck driver and was at home only on occasion, a fact Fiona didn't seem to mind. She was happy to see him when he came home, and happy for him when he left, because, as she put it, "It would be like trying to cage a wild mustang. Wade'd wither and die if he couldn't feel those big wheels rolling under him on the highway." She was the perfect mate for her man.

"You didn't have to wait around," Roger said.

"Nothing else to do," she claimed, but Roger knew she kept busy in her free time with numerous volunteer activities. "You've had a couple of calls. Both personal," she said, handing him two message slips. "I took advantage of being here on a day when the clinic was closed to start on that old storage closet in back. I'm still only halfway through, but I've fig-ured out why Dr. Stewart always kept the door locked. He didn't want me to see what a mess the place was in. He was afraid I might quit like his other assistants. Boxes piled this way and that, stacks of papers, samples. I even found a couple of missing files!"

"He told me not to worry about what was in there," Roger said. "That it wasn't important."

Fiona laughed. "He didn't want you to see, either! But didn't he think that would make us curious?"

"You were very brave to go in there alone," Roger teased.

Fiona slipped into her jacket. "Bravery is when I open that door again the next time. Lord knows what's left.'' She came out from behind the desk, tying a colorful print scarf around her neck. ''Serra was out about a half hour ago and she's been fed. You sounded tired when you called in. I thought you might not feel like doing it yourself.''

''I'm tired, but not that tired. Thanks anyway, though. I could have gotten tied up again. Wouldn't be the first time.''

''I thought about that, too.''

Roger opened the front door for her. She paused on the threshold. ''By the way, your sister sounded upset when she phoned. Just wanted you to know.''

Roger frowned at the call slips. When he looked up, Fiona had already reached her car.

With studied care he closed the door. Melissa had called, sounding upset. So what else was new? Ever since their mother had moved to Chicago to be near her, his sister had gone into frequent emotional tail-spins.

He looked at the second message as he made his way to the stairs. Raine Atwood had called as well, inviting him to dinner on Friday. A much more pleasant prospect than having to deal with his sister.

Upstairs, he took a few minutes to greet Serra before sprawling in his favorite chair and reaching for the telephone. After two rings Raine answered.

''Hey, Raine,'' he murmured.

As members of one of those strangely configured family groups that divorce and remarriage can make, he and Raine Atwood, née Peterson, had four years ago found themselves to be stepbrother and stepsister. They'd become good friends before the marriage of her mother and his father, during the time both had spent in New York—Raine as a dancer trying to make it on the Broadway stage, and Roger as a med student, trying to do as his father insisted and become a doctor. As often as they could they'd gotten together at some greasy spoon for lunch, two emigrés from Tyler in the big city.

The fact of their parents' marriage had been difficult for both of them, particularly in light of the gossip both knew must be ricocheting around Tyler. The breakup of Roger's parents' marriage, their subsequent divorce, George's courtship of Marge Peterson, then their marriage…the whole soap opera had surely kept the Tyler phone lines humming. But that was all in the past, as was Roger's own struggle between following his heart and trying to please his father.

"Is the invitation still on for Friday night?" he asked.

"Of course," Raine said.

"Can I bring a date?" He heard her short intake of breath and laughed. "Is that the baby kicking? Or shock that I might actually want to bring someone?" He could see Raine in his mind's eye—eight months pregnant and bloomingly beautiful. Copper red hair, huge green eyes and so much in love with Gabe, her new husband, that Roger sometimes felt like an intruder if he visited them for longer than fifteen minutes.

"Of course you can bring a date! Who is it?"

"A lady I met this weekend."

"At the dog show? Roger, this *is* a person we're

talking about, isn't it? I mean, you haven't gone completely weird and—''

"It's entirely possible that she won't come," he said. "I'm not exactly in her good books at the moment. She thinks I insulted her."

"Roger! You?"

"I opened my mouth and something fell out that shouldn't have."

"Tell me. Who is she?" Raine probed.

"The lady will remain anonymous unless and until she comes with me Friday night. Either way, I'll be there."

Raine groaned in frustration.

"How's Gabe?" he asked.

"Working hard."

"And you?"

She laughed. "Ready for this baby to be born. Then again," she added soberly, "a little afraid. It's going to be an awsome responsibility to be a parent."

"At least you have Gabe to help you."

"Yes," she said softly, "I have Gabe."

He sat forward. "What time on Friday?"

"Eight o'clock sound good to you?"

"I'll be there. Oh, and I'll let you know about the date."

"You don't have to," she said. "Just bring her along." She sighed. "You know, you have really tweaked my curiosity."

"Good!" he replied in a pleased voice. Then he hung up.

Roger's second call was made with far less enthusiasm. While he waited for the telephone at his sister's house to be answered, the muscles in his stomach tightened.

Melissa was one year his senior. She'd been married for almost ten years, had two boys, ages six and eight, plus a husband who adored her, and still she managed to be disgruntled about almost everything. "She's too much like you!" Roger had once overheard his father complain to his mother when they were having one of their tightly controlled arguments. "She's too worried about what others think. Her nose is almost as high in the air as yours is!" The accusation hadn't endeared his father to him, even though it had been accurate.

"Hello?" Melissa's tense voice spoke in his ear. He could almost feel the anger vibrating within her.

Bracing himself, he asked, "What's up, sis?"

"He's doing it again," she said tightly. "Roger, you have to make him stop! I've tried. I just hang up on him when he calls. But he calls right back. It's starting to drive me insane!"

"He just wants to talk to the kids, Missy."

"Well, he's not going to! When he divorced Mom, he divorced me, too. And my children. If Mom wasn't good enough for him anymore, neither are we. Now he 'misses his grandchildren.'" She did a fairly good imitation of their father. "Well, maybe he should have thought of that before he took up with that— that…"

"Now, Missy," Roger said soothingly, "it isn't good for you to be so angry all the time."

"How can I not be?" she demanded. "How can *you* not be? He's your father, too. And Mom is your mother! How can you not stand up for her? You should come visit her more often, Roger, then you'd see. She still wanders around, looking lost...."

"Mother's stronger than you think," Roger said quietly.

"But she's not! She's not! She's over here every day, telling me—"

"Take a deep breath, Missy. Now another. How long has it been since you've had a check-up?"

"You sound just like *him!*" she accused.

"Getting sick isn't going to help you, Mom or your kids. You have to take care of yourself."

"Are you going to talk to him?" she demanded, dismissing what he'd said.

Roger sighed. He loved his mother just as much as Melissa did, but he saw her a little more clearly. He knew how difficult she had been to live with, with her driving need to stay ahead of everyone else, to be the leader of Tyler society. She'd been so proud to be the wife of the chief of staff at Tyler General. She seemed to love the exalted position more than she loved their father. Not that Roger was making excuses for their dad. He'd cut the marital cord a little too callously, from Roger's point of view.

"I'll talk to him," he promised.

"Good," she said, sounding relieved but not relaxed.

"Missy, it's been four years," Roger ventured. "Mom should be getting on with her life, not—"

"How can she, when he hurt her so terribly?"

"Has she joined any kind of group or club? She used to be on almost every committee in Tyler, chaired more than a few of them. She needs to get out, see people, get involved again. Maybe that would help.'' *And then she'd leave you alone,* Roger added to himself.

"Why don't you come tell her that? She's always listened to you more than me.''

Roger rubbed the bridge of his nose. "She doesn't listen to me, either," he said flatly.

"That's what you think!''

Roger sighed. This was the way all his conversations ended with Melissa. She always found something to blame him for.

"Listen, Missy. I have to go check on my patients. I'll talk with Dad tomorrow, see if I can get him to cool it with the phone calls. But I'm telling you, it wouldn't hurt for you to be reasonable, too. For the kids' sake. A granddad is a good thing for a boy to have.''

"Not this granddad. Anyway, they have another. John's father.''

John's father—the president of a huge manufacturing company. Big house, big paycheck, firm standing in the Chicago business community. Roger wondered why their mother hadn't latched on to his coattails to gain entry into society there. Then he instantly regretted the unworthy thought.

"I'll try to get down to see you and Mom soon,'' he promised, but he couldn't help hoping that the day could be put off.

He made no motion to rise after hanging up. As he'd told Missy, he needed to see to his patients downstairs, but he couldn't get his mind off the strife that still tore at his family.

Somehow he and his father had managed to forge a new relationship. Roger tried hard not hold grudges or to judge, and so did his father. George had even come to accept his son's switch to veterinary medicine, which was a miracle, considering the past.

Since his marriage to Marge Peterson, George Phelps had undergone a number of changes. He was far more relaxed, far happier. If Melissa could only talk to him from outside the filter of their mother's continuing anger, she might see… Yeah, and if a frog had wings it wouldn't bump its butt on the ground when it hopped!

Roger pushed tiredly out of the chair and, with Serra at his side, he went to minister to his charges. There were times, he admitted, when he felt more like a hundred than twenty-eight. When he'd told Gracie Lawson that he'd always been mature for his age, he hadn't lied. He'd been born a peacemaker. Either that or he'd learned the knack quickly in a house where icy silences between his parents passed for everyday life.

He shook his head, dispelling the negative memory. It was far better to let his thoughts dwell on Gracie Lawson.

A pleased smile touched his lips as he rounded the base of the stairs. She might take issue with the idea, but he knew that something electrical pulsed in the air between them. Something that was well worth exploring.

He stepped into the room lined with spacious cages

for unwell animals, and Serra stopped at the door. He'd needed to direct her only once not to come into the room, and she never did. He'd made the rule for her safety, as well as to keep the room's occupants from being disturbed.

By force of habit, Roger slipped into the white lab coat he wore while on duty, and eyed the waiting dog. "It's been a long time since you were in here yourself, hasn't it, girl? Do you remember? You were a pretty sick little lady. But look at you now...you're beautiful!"

Serra gazed at him, her sherry-colored eyes serious, almost as if she were remembering. Then her long, feathery tail began to swish, and the look in her eyes resolved into love.

Roger moved toward her and squatted down. He stroked her head, and her eyes grew even warmer. "A man and his dog," he murmured. "Or should it be a dog and her man? I sometimes wonder who owns who."

Serra made a noise deep in her throat.

"You say you like the last best?" he teased. "Maybe I should get you to have a little talk with another lady I know. You can tell her that I'm not such a bad person."

Serra did something then that she hadn't done since the first night he'd known her. Nudging his hand out of the way, she lifted her muzzle and gave his chin a soft lick.

Roger sat back on his heels. "Was that a yes?" he asked, but he said it through a suddenly tight throat. He'd been the recipient of many dog kisses over the years, a few from cats, even one or two from cows. But of all he'd ever received, none touched his heart in the same way as Serra's did. Serra, who had so little reason in her life to show affection to a member of the human race.

CHAPTER FIVE

GRACIE HUNG the last of her collection of blue-willow plates on the white clapboard wall, centering it between the front windows. It amazed her how fast she'd been able to make this tiny temporary home comfortable. Her furnishings, a number of which had come down to her from her mother, fitted as if made for it. Space was limited, but the country look she loved worked perfectly here.

Jacques and Jo-Jo watched her raptly, one on either end of the couch.

Gracie leaned back to survey her handiwork. "Looks good, doesn't it?" she asked the boys. "Darned right, it does," she answered for them. "Just like home."

She put the hammer and spare nails away, checked the pot of stew simmering on the stove, then went back into the living room just in time to hear the clock on the mantel give three chimes. Only three o'clock.

Gracie restlessly sank into the flowery chair that matched the sofa. She'd been struggling since noon to find things to do. At Grace Farms she wouldn't be having this problem. There weren't enough hours in a day to accomplish everything that needed to be done. Grace Farms... Her heart gave a little squeeze. She missed it!

Then again, she didn't. She knew she'd done the right thing in selling the kennel. Something was basically wrong in life when a person gave herself over so exclusively to one thing that there was room for nothing else, not even friends and family. Such isolation wasn't healthy.

It had happened to her before she'd known it. Little by little after her breakup with Paul, she had pulled away, not accepting invitations, not returning calls. Her life had revolved around her numerous dogs. Because they could be trusted not to hurt her? She hadn't even seen it when Emil had gone through his trouble, after Myrna died. Realization came afterward, when she recalled telling Sheilie that she'd have to schedule in a time to see him. Schedule in a time to see her ailing only brother? Gracie had made a long, hard examination of her situation at that point and had decided to make some big changes.

Unpacking boxes and settling in had taken most of her time up to now, not to mention helping with the dog show. She'd worked long and hard, ensuring that everything was just right. But the dog show was over and the last of the boxes had been recycled. Now she had to figure out what to do next.

The doorbell rang, and glad for a diversion, she went to answer it.

Her niece's bright and smiling face greeted her.

"Surprise, it's me!" Sheila cried. "I have the afternoon free and I couldn't think of a better thing to do than spend part of it with my favorite aunt!"

"Douglas is at a teacher's meeting, right?" Gracie guessed.

Sheila laughed at being caught out. "Right."

"Well, come on in anyway, even if I am second best."

Jo-Jo bounced over to greet Sheila, while Jacques waited on the sofa. Gracie felt her niece's sharp gaze when she straightened from greeting the dogs.

"So," Sheila said brightly. "How did it go?"

"How did what go?" Gracie asked. She made a pretense of considering the alignment of the blue-willow plates, as if one was off balance. "Don't those plates look nice over there? I love these rustic walls." She paused. "Is something wrong with the plate on the far left?"

"Your trip home last night." Sheila stuck to the subject. "Has Roger persuaded you to go out with him yet?"

Gracie gave the plate a small adjustment. Not for a second was she going to look at her niece; Sheila's intuition was far too good. "No," she said, then tried to change the subject. "Has the hotel had any trouble recovering from the dog show? I suppose that funny little man is finally happy, now that we're gone."

"I know what you're doing, Aunt Grace, so your little ploy isn't going to work. At least, it wouldn't work if I didn't have something very interesting to tell you…since you mentioned the little man."

That finally gained Gracie's full attention. She turned to look at her niece.

Sheila settled on the couch and patted the seat

cushion. "Come sit down," she said. "This is going to take awhile."

"My goodness, what is it?" Gracie asked, complying.

Sheila reached into her purse and brought out a folded sheet of paper. "Read this," she said, handing it over. "It's a copy of a fax that arrived this morning."

Gracie frowned. "A fax?" She frowned even more when she saw that the fax was addressed to Angus Watson. "Isn't this—?"

Sheila nodded. "Our funny little man. Only there may be more to him than that. Go on, read it."

"Is it legal to… I mean, isn't it something like reading someone else's mail?"

"Brick Bauer himself asked me to watch out for any communication coming from Palm Beach, Florida, or southern California. Look at the top of the page. It's 407—that's the Palm Beach area code."

"Brick?" Gracie echoed. "Why would Brick—"

"I'll tell you after you read it, okay?"

Gracie focused on the paper in her hand. The note was in a firm but sprawling hand, as if whoever had written it was in a hurry. *My shipment has yet to arrive. Why not? My patience is growing thin. Either find D.S. soon, or I'll take my business elsewhere!* And it was signed, *C.H.*

"This C.H. sounds like an unhappy customer," Gracie said. "What kind of business is our man in?"

"What else? Funny business."

Gracie dropped the letter to her lap. "Sheila, stop

it! Make sense. What in the world…*why* in the world would Brick—''

''I'd have thought she was an irate customer, too, and would have passed the fax on to Mr. Watson without another thought. But there's more going on here than meets the eye. C.H. isn't an ordinary customer. She's a woman named Celeste Huntington, and the D.S. is Daphne Sullivan. And the 'shipment' is Daphne's baby, Jenny.''

''Who's Daphne Sullivan?'' Gracie asked. ''Someone new in Tyler?''

''She's been here for almost a year. She's Judy Lowery's half sister, though hardly anyone knows that. Have you heard of Judy, the mystery writer?'' When Gracie nodded, Sheila continued, ''It seems Celeste Huntington is Daphne's mother-in-law. She has bags of money and doesn't want Daphne to raise her own baby. She wants to take Jenny away.''

''How did you learn all this?'' Gracie asked, aghast.

''From Brick. He's pretty tight-lipped—a typical policeman—but I managed to get some information out of him. And I put a few things together myself. I knew the fax was important when he read it. His shoulders tensed and he looked really grim. He didn't want to say anything at first, but when I told him I'd ask Mr. Watson about it, you should have seen him shoot out of his chair! He didn't want me to do that at all!''

''Sheilie, you have to be careful,'' Gracie cautioned. ''This Mr. Watson—''

''Must be some kind of hired thug! We knew there

was something funny about him. You and I picked up on it right away. No wonder he can't play golf! It's all a cover to get Daphne's baby."

"Sheilie, you aren't going to—"

"Ask him about it? No, I promised Brick I wouldn't. But I am going to watch him for as long as he stays at the hotel. Brick wants me to continue keeping an eye out for communication from Celeste Huntington. I'm to let him know right away if something comes in."

"Are you going to tell Douglas what you're doing? He won't like it. He'll worry."

"I know he won't like it. That's why I'm telling you instead."

"So I'll know what's happened if you suddenly disappear? Sheilie!"

Sheila laughed as she stood up. "I'm not going to disappear. Daphne's the one who did that—did I tell you? *She* disappeared a couple of weeks ago. She used to work at the Yes! Yogurt shop—I'd usually see her on my day off. Britt's telling anyone who asks that Daphne and this new guy she's met, Vic Estevez—I doubt you'd know him because I don't know him, either!—were getting pretty serious, and Vic took her and little Jenny home to meet his parents in California. *Now,* I wonder if that's true. If they're in California, why is Angus Watson here? And why is Celeste Huntington sending angry messages to him?"

Gracie got slowly to her feet. "Just be careful, okay? You're the only niece I have."

Sheila grinned. "I'll be careful if you'll promise *not* to be. Give Roger a chance! Don't be such a stick-in-the-mud.'' Sheila leaned close and kissed Gracie's cheek. "Now, I have to get going. Douglas's meeting should be over and I promised I'd pick him up."

When Gracie turned from closing the front door, the clock on the mantel chimed the half hour. For that short period, time had gone by in a flash. Now all she had to do was get through the rest of the day.

ANGUS WATSON MADE two telephone calls that morning after getting the kick-in-the-butt message from Celeste Huntington. The first was to a local realty office, asking about rental properties. He was particularly interested in a farm he'd heard was available. He'd already driven by it and thought it perfect for his needs, since it belonged to a local woman named Judy Lowery. The Realtor fell all over herself setting up an appointment for a closer viewing.

The second call went to Celeste Huntington. Mercifully, he reached her answering machine and was able to leave word that he was on top of the situation and would soon be changing his base of operation, the better to infiltrate the local scene.

His next act was to drive into Tyler, to the genteel department store on the town square that looked as if it had been serving customers for several generations. He went directly to the men's-wear department and completely changed his look. He shed the skin of an avid golfing enthusiast, opting for one more in keeping with a lord-of-the-manor theme. He kept to wool jackets, but these had leather elbow patches, and the slacks went all the way down to his shoes. He covered his receding hairline with a jaunty hat sporting a small red feather.

He preened before the mirror, rocking back and forth on his feet and curled his fingers around the lapels. Yes, he decided, the look was perfect.

He unrolled a wad of cash to pay for the outfit and planted one of the first seeds of the story he wanted to circulate. "Tyler is exactly what I've been looking for for years," he enthused to the salesclerk. "A perfect place to breathe fresh air, get the feel of the land." Then he went off to the realty office.

The real-estate agent, when they met face-to-face, seemed convinced by his new persona. "I'm sure we'll find exactly what you're looking for, Mr. Watson," she gushed. "If the Lowery farm isn't it, I have other properties. Not quite as large in acreage, but just as nice."

Angus nodded, letting her think he might be interested in other spots, when his goal, already set when he'd first called her, was to rent the Lowery farm. It tickled his fancy that he, one of the gang that had come so close to carrying out Celeste Huntington's wishes—to wrench the screaming child out of its mother's arms, if need be—would live on the farm where his quarry had once taken cover. Who would think he'd have that much gall? And who knew? Maybe he'd find a clue to her present whereabouts in one of the farm's nooks and crannies. Daphne Sullivan hadn't had a lot of time to pack before she'd run away.

He was like a hound on the scent, he decided happily as he followed the agent out to the farm in his silver Buick. It wasn't his place to feel sorry for the kid or for the kid's mother. His loyalty went to the person who paid his meal ticket. And right now that was Celeste Huntington.

It also wasn't his job to ask unnecessary questions or to pass judgment. He'd already confirmed a lot of the information he'd been given, and added more. He knew that Judy Lowery, Daphne's half sister, was a writer working out of her home in Tyler. He knew that Vic Estevez, his predecessor on the job—an ex-cop who had turned soft and helped Daphne and her child get away—had become good friends with the publisher of the local rag, Rob Friedman. Angus was also aware that Britt Marshack, who lived on the farm closest to the one they were approaching, was close friends with Judy Lowery and had become friendly with her sister, to the point of employing Daphne in her new yogurt shop in town. *And* that Britt Marshack's husband, Jake, was also a friend of Rob Friedman. Celeste was convinced that one or all of them knew where Daphne, Vic and the child had gone. Angus was, too.

As he stepped out of the car at the Lowery farm he affected a pleased smile. ''Wonderful, wonderful,'' he murmured.

The Realtor beamed at him. She took him through the house, a rather plain, generic farm house, and on a tour of the outbuildings.

Angus had to work hard not to hoot with laughter when she pointed to a pen and proudly proclaimed that it once had housed the goats whose milk had been used to make the first samples of Yes! Yogurt.

"Britt Marshack lives next door," she said. "She came up with the idea for the yogurt and made it in her kitchen. She did so well that now it's this huge business. Not that she runs the operation out of her kitchen any longer. Yes! Yogurt has become so successful they had to move to larger facilities." She took a quick breath upon realizing her gaff. "But there's nothing to disturb your peace and quiet here. The factory's down the road...*way* down the road. Britt and Jake Marshack...have you met them? I can introduce you. They're *very* nice people. I'm sure they'd be glad to give you a tour of the plant...the plant that's down the road."

Angus couldn't keep his lips from twitching. *Really came close to stepping in that one, didn't you?* he thought. *You're backing up like a crawfish out of its hole! If I was a normal client looking for peace and quiet, you could easily have lost yourself a customer.*

"I understand what you're saying," he said levelly. "My own business started small and quickly outgrew its first building. I had to move from a place in town to one on the outskirts, where we'd have more room."

"Your business?" she echoed, showing more real interest than she had before.

"I make plumbing fixtures," he lied. "Unique Fixtures for Unique Homes...that's my motto. I made it up myself. I like to think that people appreciate quality. And they sure seem to. I have sinks and tubs in houses throughout the Midwest."

"Oh, my," the Realtor twittered.

"It got to the point," he continued as they started back to their cars, "that I was able to pull out of the day-to-day operation of the business and leave it to my second-in-command. I had a spell of bad health a few years ago. The doctor told me I worked too hard, that I should take more time off. I'm taking him at his word.''

"A very wise thing to do,'' she agreed.

"I only go in once or twice a year now to check up on things.''

She gave a girlish giggle even though she must be in her late thirties. She was a strawberry blonde—out of the bottle Angus suspected—and more than a little overweight. But she still managed to look attractive. Her clothes were nice and she paid attention to her grooming.

"And the name of your business?'' she inquired.

Angus faked fumbling with his sunglasses so he wouldn't have to answer. A moment later he nodded as he looked around at the gently rolling pastures. "Yes, I think I'm going to like this place. I might even decide to make an offer on it if the owner's interested.''

That really got her going. The prospect of a sale acted like an aphrodisiac. "Judy didn't say if she was interested in selling, but I'll check. I'll talk to her just as soon as I get back to the office!''

"You do that,'' Angus agreed.

He slid back into the silver Buick and gave a friendly wave before heading for the highway.

As he drove away he congratulated himself on handling the situation perfectly.

ROGER LEFT his father's house at the intersection of Morgan Avenue and Second Street. He'd arrived shortly after dinner and had stayed for over an hour. Marge had insisted that he have a piece of her special carrot cake, and Roger, being of sound mind—Marge was an excellent cook—agreed.

After dinner, probably sensing that Roger had something to discuss with his father, Marge went to visit Raine and Gabe at their new home a few streets away. They'd lived there for a month now and were busy decorating the nursery. She said she wanted to check the day's progress.

From that point, Roger had proceeded delicately, doing the best he could to get Melissa's message across without inflicting unnecessary pain. His father was extremely sensitive about his deteriorated relationship with his only daughter.

"Just give her a little space," Roger had advised. "Don't push."

"If I don't push there won't be any communication between us at all! I can't just let her slip away, Roger," George had replied.

"Is that what you call communication? Hearing her hang up?"

His father had looked away, his jaw tight.

"Just…give it a rest for a few weeks, Dad. That's all. Then—"

"Then it can start all over again? This is your mother's fault, Roger. You know that. She's the one causing the trouble."

"Mom's not very happy, Dad."

"She never was," George had snapped. Then he'd run a hand through his graying hair. For a moment he'd slipped back into the man he used to be—distant, demanding, unforgiving. He attempted a rueful smile and murmured, "More's the pity for her. I truly do feel sorry for her sometimes, son. You believe that, don't you?"

"I do," Roger said. It seemed very important to his father that he acknowledge that.

"Now, if I could only get Missy to see it." George sighed.

After their talk, Roger stood on the abbreviated front porch to the house his father shared with Marge and burrowed deeper into his leather jacket. The fall evenings were starting to have a decided nip. Crisp, cool, crystalline air with delicate wisps of fireplace smoke, piles of newly raked leaves, a full moon so close it seemed all you had to do was reach out and touch it... He loved this time of year almost as much as he loved the spring.

He descended the single step to the walkway, then turned automatically down the sidewalk toward home. After only a few yards, though, he stopped. The situation between his father and his sister frustrated him because there was little he could do to improve it. But something much more promising beckoned from nearby. Or rather, some*one*. He pivoted and proceeded in the opposite direction.

Three blocks later he stopped again. Lights were on in the small wood-frame house at the corner of Morgan and Fifth. How would Grace Lawson react if he just showed up?

He rang the doorbell and waited. He could hear

activity inside the house—a voice, a barking dog. Then the fast approach of footsteps.

"Yes?" she said as she swung the door open. She wore a full apron that was too large for her—the bib string was knotted in a loop at the back of her neck, the skirt hung down past her jeans-clad knees, the tie at the waist was wrapped around twice. In her hand was a grooming brush. "Oh, it's you!" she said. Roger couldn't tell if she was pleased or dismayed to see him.

"Am I interrupting?" he asked, when he knew very well that he was. Tufts of freshly cut black poodle hair clung to the front of the apron and a clump was stuck to one shoe.

"Oh, no," she answered breathlessly. And a touch wryly? "I'm not doing a thing."

A little black poodle came running from the rear of the house, barking excitedly all the way, while barks and whines erupted from a dog who couldn't make the trip.

"Jacques, be quiet!" she called over her shoulder. "Jo-Jo," she admonished the dog dancing frantically at her feet, "you, too!"

Roger bent down and scooped the eight or nine pounds of squirming dog into his arms, then with practiced ease he folded him against his body. "Be a good boy, Jo-Jo," he directed into the bright little button-black eyes, while stroking the dog's head. Jo-Jo instantly relaxed.

Jacques continued to whine and bark and plead.

"You want to go see to him?" Roger asked.

Gracie turned on her heels, and Roger followed her down a narrow hall.

The second poodle stood on a grooming table, held in place by a restraining loop. This dog had some years on him, Roger saw instantly. His muzzle was laced with white hairs, and his eyes weren't as bright and enthusiastic as Jo-Jo's. He barked, but he didn't move a paw, he was so well trained for grooming.

"Hello, Jacques," Roger greeted him, running his free hand over the little dog's body, instinctively performing a quick examination. The dog was almost finished with his clip. His face and paws were cut to velvet, his body and leg hair left longer in what was called a kennel cut. Even more loose tufts of curly black hair festooned the table and the floor.

Jacques wagged his tail at Roger, happy to greet him. The poof of hair on the crown of his head was only partially sculpted.

"You're almost done," Roger observed, speaking to Gracie.

"With one," she said. "Jo-Jo's next."

Instead of resuming her work, though, she hovered on the opposite side of the grooming table. Using it as a barrier? Roger wondered. Did she think he was about to lunge at her, to continue what he had started the evening before?

"They're beautiful dogs," Roger said. "Happy, healthy…"

He'd said the wrong thing. She instantly bristled. "Is that what you came to check?" she demanded. "How I care for my dogs? I thought you said you didn't think I was irresponsible. Have you changed your mind?''

Roger took a deep breath. He couldn't seem to get off on the right foot with her. Whatever he said, she turned it into a thrust and parry. "I came to ask if you'd like to have dinner with me on Friday," he said quietly. "At Raine and Gabe Atwood's. They told me to bring a guest."

She was shaking her head before he finished. "Find someone else."

"I don't want to."

"And I don't want to go."

Roger looked at her for a long moment, remembering the warmth of her response when they'd kissed. There was something there that had caused feelings to flare between them. Denying it couldn't make it go away, although she seemed determined to. Why? Was it the age thing? Or did it have to do with the snippets of gossip he'd picked up at the dog show? Something about a relationship that had dissolved in a very public way.

"Think about it," he advised, giving her a soft smile. Then he rubbed Jacques's head again, placed Jo-Jo back on the floor and retreated into the hall. "I'll let myself out," he called.

FOR GRACIE, those unexpected few minutes with Roger Phelps melded with the surreal happenings of the past several days. He'd just rung the bell and walked in as if assured that he was completely welcome, then he'd invited her to share a meal with his friends, after which he'd left.

She blinked in confusion. Why was he doing this? Why had he fixated on her when there were so many other women out there who would undoubtedly welcome his attention? He was decidedly attractive, got on well with animals and humans alike, had a keen sense of humor and a wry sense of fun. *Why her?*

Gracie stood with her hands braced on the edge of the grooming table, while Jo-Jo, balanced on his hind legs, clawed at her jeans, wanting to be picked up. Jacques, for his part, wagged his tail and waited.

"You weren't much help," she scolded them both, looking from one to the other. "You liked him, didn't you?"

The answer they gave wasn't the one she wanted.

CHAPTER SIX

GRACIE WAS A WOMAN of fierce determination. And when she decided that she had to start making a new life for herself, she did it with verve. Never before had she had the luxury of time. Now that she did, she wanted to join every volunteer group that interested her. It would get her out among people, let her help out in the community and also would fill the hours of her day. And maybe, after some time had passed, it would help give direction to the next stage of her life. Help her center in on what she wanted to do.

Meals on Wheels needed drivers to make deliveries to shut-ins. Elder Services needed people to make daily contact telephone calls. The library needed someone to read to children twice a week. The animal shelter in Sugar Creek was in desperate need of help, and a pet-therapy group was looking for new members to visit care facilities. Within a few days of making contacts, Gracie had set up an active schedule.

She was just getting out of her car, which she'd parked near the town square, on her way to pick up her list of Elder Services names and telephone numbers, when Brick Bauer saw her and called her aside.

A law-abiding citizen her entire life, Gracie was startled to be the object of police attention, even a policeman she'd been marginally acquainted with for years. It must be the uniform that intimidated her, she thought as she responded to his request. Also, the badge, the gun holstered on his hip, the look of purposeful intent written on his face and in his eyes.

Her mind went over the last few minutes. She'd signaled her turn; she wasn't parked illegally in a handicapped zone; she hadn't been speeding....

Brick was a handsome man, solidly built. If a wrongdoer wanted trouble, the police captain could give it to him.

"Ms. Lawson," he said formally.

"Yes?" Gracie answered, trying to sound assured.

"I wonder if I might have a word with you. Privately," he added at her continued look of confusion.

Gracie's worry expanded to include the past day, the past week. "Certainly," she agreed, still coming up with nothing.

He motioned her into the grassy square and over to a park bench, where they sat down. Very few people were taking advantage of the square that morning, though the nearby shops and offices were bustling.

As Gracie waited for Brick to proceed, a brightly colored maple leaf fluttered to the ground to join a number of others.

"Sheila tells me she spoke with you about Angus Watson," Brick said at last. "And that she showed you the fax."

"Yes, she did," Gracie confirmed.

"Well, I'd appreciate it if you wouldn't tell anyone about it. It concerns a matter under investigation. You haven't, have you?"

"No."

"Good," he said, relaxing enough to smile slightly. Then he stood up. "The fewer people who know about this the better—for now."

"I won't say a word," Gracie promised.

He nodded and moved away.

Gracie stayed where she was, her mind again racing, only this time along a different course. This Angus Watson business must be serious for Brick Bauer to track her down and warn her off. Her concern for Sheila grew. She hoped her niece would behave sensibly, wouldn't take any risks. As soon as Gracie got home, she'd call and remind her of her pledge to use caution.

"Are we going to see your face up on a Wanted poster any time soon?" A teasing voice intruded upon Gracie's thoughts.

She didn't have to look around to know who it was. Her body's instant response gave its own clue. "Why do you say that?" she asked.

"Brick Bauer seemed rather intense." Roger took Brick's place on the bench.

"He just wanted to ask me a question."

After a moment Roger said, "This is Friday. You still haven't told me if you'll come tonight."

Gracie shook her head. "I did tell you. I said no."

"And I asked you to think about it."

"I have."

"I want to get to know you, Grace."

Gracie stood up. "You'll get over it."

"What if I don't?" he challenged.

She looked around, checking to see if anyone was

watching. They were in the Tyler town square, after all. "You *will*," she said emphatically, then turned to go back to her car. Her original plan to collect the needed telephone numbers was no longer her top priority. Getting away from him was. Getting away from the confusion he brought with him.

Why did she react to him as she did? She was almost forty, experienced in life. And she'd paid very dearly for that experience. A palpitating heart and suddenly weak knees were symptoms of a schoolgirl!

"What are you running away from, Grace?" Roger called softly after her from where she'd left him sitting on the bench.

She hurried on. At least this time he didn't follow her.

ROGER WAS LATE for his dinner engagement that evening. Someone had called the clinic in a panic because his dog had gotten loose and been hit by a car, the same someone who had come in twice before over the last few months with an identical complaint.

Both prior times the dog had been lucky. This time, too much damage had been done, and Roger had been unable to save it. The owner had gone into an emotional collapse, and it was all Roger could do to show compassion.

When he finally arrived at Raine and Gabe's house, he could feel tension knotting the muscles in his neck and shoulders and a hammer pounding in his head.

Raine took one look at him and led him to a chair. "Gabe!" she called into the kitchen. "Bring the coffee. Roger is in dire need."

A tall, thin, nice-looking man only a couple of years older than Roger came into the room carrying a glass carafe of freshly brewed coffee. "Never let it be said that I shirked in my duty," he said as he poured a measure into one of the waiting cups.

The marriage of Gabe Atwood and Raine Peterson last spring had been one of the nine-day wonders of Tyler. Rumor and speculation had swirled, made even more intense by the uncertainty surrounding the paternity of Raine's expected baby. Was the father Gabe, or someone Raine had met while living in New York? Had Gabe married her only because they were childhood friends and he'd always made it a habit to look after her?

Roger had to confess that when he'd first heard the news, he'd wondered, too. Not once during the times he and Raine had met for lunch while both of them were living in New York had she mentioned Gabe other than in passing, as a friend. Then, out of the blue, she'd married him. To see them together now, though, allowed no question about the depth of their love. It was there in the way they looked at each other, their deep need for contact—the touch of a hand, a shared smile—when they'd been apart for too long.

Raine was eight months pregnant. Only a short time remained until the baby's birth, and if Gabe wasn't the blood father, he gave no indication of resentment or jealousy. He was just as anxious for the birth as Raine, just as welcoming of the child.

"A firefighter should never shirk his duty," Roger murmured, accepting the cup.

Raine perched on the ottoman at Roger's feet. "What happened?" she asked gently. "Was it something at work or—"

"A dog died. I couldn't do anything for him."

"Oh, no."

"He'd been hit by a car. His third time wasn't a charm." Roger rubbed the back of his neck, while Gabe came up behind Raine to rest his hands on her shoulders. Roger continued, "The owner wouldn't repair his fence. The dog kept getting out. They lived next to a busy intersection...." He shrugged. "The owner's distraught now, as well he should be. It was all I could do not to punch him out. I warned him the last time...." Roger sighed. "Sorry, this isn't something you should have to hear."

Raine leaned forward to take his hand. "It's better for you to talk about it."

Roger looked up into Gabe's pale blue eyes. Gabe was one of the most genuinely nice people Roger knew. And his protectiveness of Raine had been lifelong. If Roger had gone too far, enough to upset Raine, Gabe would let him know. Roger saw no condemnation.

"It was the poor dog who paid the highest price," Raine said regretfully.

Roger's jaw tightened. "If I had my way some people wouldn't be allowed to have pets."

The room was silent, Gabe and Raine allowing Roger time to recover. Finally, he noticed a tantalizing aroma. His nose twitched.

"What's for dinner?" he asked.

"Grilled salmon fillets, riced potatoes and almond carrots. Sound good?" Raine asked jauntily.

"M-m-m," Roger replied.

Gabe sat down to pour himself a cup of coffee and refill Roger's cup. Raine limited herself to fruit juice.

She took a sip and smiled. "So," she said, "tell us who the mystery lady is. Are you still in her bad books? Is that why she refused your invitation?"

Roger grimaced. "I'm in her bad books so far I'm not sure I'll ever get out."

"Raine's been guessing all week," Gabe said.

Roger hesitated, then he asked, "Do you remember Gracie Lawson?"

Raine frowned. "*Gracie* Lawson?" she repeated.

"She bred and showed toy poodles and had a kennel in the country. She's just recently moved back to Tyler."

"Sheila's aunt!" Raine exclaimed. "Yes, I remember her."

"Her," Roger said.

Raine didn't connect. She still looked at him expectantly, waiting for him to divulge the name.

"Her," Roger repeated. "Gracie's the woman I asked to dinner."

Raine blinked. "Gracie Lawson?" she said.

Gabe rubbed his chin and smiled. "I remember her, too. Not bigger than a minute, but with an *amazing* shape."

"Gabe!" Raine scolded him.

Gabe laughed. "Well, it was pretty amazing. Curves in all the right places. Some of my track buddies in high school used to alter their practice route through town so they could run by her house, hoping to see her. She was older, but that only added to the allure.''

"She still looks the same," Roger murmured.

"Curves still in all the right places?" Gabe asked, teasing his wife.

"Definitely," Roger agreed.

Raine reached for a pillow and thumped each of them.

"Did you run by her house?" Raine demanded of her husband. "Did you?"

"I can't remember," Gabe evaded, chuckling.

"I was her bag boy at the supermarket," Roger volunteered. "I made sure everything was perfect—not too heavy, not too bulky."

"I never knew you were a bag boy," Raine said.

"A misadventure of my youth," Roger explained.

Raine stopped laughing and looked carefully at her stepbrother. "You really do like her," she said with dawning perception.

"I really do, yes," Roger agreed.

"What did you say to insult her?"

"I didn't mean to. It just—"

"Fell out. I know, you told me."

"She thinks I think she's an irresponsible breeder."

Raine blinked. "That doesn't sound very good. How is a breeder irresponsible?" she asked.

"In this context, by inbreeding. It causes all kinds of problems. Hip dysplasia, muscular dystrophy, bleeding disorders, skin and temperament problems—"

"Inbreeding?" Raine interrupted him. "You mean, like—"

"The best way to produce a puppy that meets the proper official standard for the breed—long ears on a Cocker Spaniel, sloping hind legs on a German Shepherd, a huge head on a Bulldog…that kind of thing—is to mate two dogs who have that trait. The closest resemblances are in families, so irresponsible breeders breed only for that. They don't care that both parents might carry a recessive gene and their pups could develop problems—are likely to develop problems. All they're interested in is turning a profit."

"You believe she's like that?" Raine said incredulously.

Roger leaned forward. "No, I don't! There are plenty of responsible breeders! People who mate their dogs with care, who work to eliminate genetic defects, or at least cut down on their occurrences. Dog clubs are funding research into genetics and altering their standards to include health as well as beauty. From all that I heard about Gracie and her breeding program, she did everything she could."

"Then why…?"

"Because when you've seen a dog suffering, it's hard not to point the finger of blame at everyone in the business. Dr. Stewart hated professional breeders. He thought each and every one of them were in it for the money, and he wasn't shy about saying so."

"But you're not Dr. Stewart."

"I still see the animals. I still get frustrated and angry when a dog is crippled unnecessarily or goes blind or…" He stopped himself again. Then, shaking his head, he said ruefully, "Now you can see why she turned me down. I'm just a bundle of laughs to be around."

"You care," Gabe said simply.

Raine smiled. "Ask her again," she encouraged him. "Use some of that patented Roger Phelps charm and she'll come around."

"I think she's immune."

"Don't give up," she insisted. "If Gabe had given up…"

Raine looked at her husband, and as he gazed back at her a spark of such intense feeling passed between them that Roger swallowed hard. Growing up, he hadn't known that a love like that could exist between a husband and wife—a love that had no boundaries. And when he'd discovered that it could, he'd wondered if it would ever happen to him. He still did.

GRACIE PLUNGED into her volunteer work, zipping from one appointment to another. On some days she groomed and exercised dogs at the shelter in Sugar Creek and played with homeless kittens. On other days she delivered lunches to the old and infirm in and around Tyler, and read Maurice Sendak and Dr. Seuss stories to five-year-olds at the library.

Keeping busy kept her from thinking—about the ups and downs in her life, about her continuing problem with Roger.…

What she knew would soon be her favorite activity took longest to set up, because it required a period of evaluation and training—for herself and for the boys. Pet Friends was an organization that carefully screened prospective members in order to provide only the best of experiences for the people they served.

Jacques, Jo-Jo and she all had to be certified. By the following Thursday they were, and they were ready to pay their first call. They and several other Pet Friends associates were to meet in the lobby of Worthington House, there to proceed to different areas of the nursing home and retirement facility. Because they were new to the program, Gracie and the boys were to work in the retirement section, visiting lonely seniors in the company of a more experienced Friend.

Gracie had no idea the Friend would turn out to be Fiona Evans. Fiona and her husband, Wade, had moved into the house next door to Gracie and her mother shortly before her mother's sudden final illness. The usual friendly overtures had been exchanged, but it wasn't until Gracie's mother's first emergency trip to the hospital that Fiona's compassionate nature had emerged. She'd done everything she could to help make Gracie's life easier, from running errands to assisting with her mother's daily nursing. She'd even been visiting when Gracie's mom had died. For a time afterward they'd remained close, but after Gracie's move to the country, they'd slowly drifted apart.

"Gracie?" Fiona exclaimed. "Is that you? I never thought…" She rushed over to deliver a huge hug.

Never one to be mistaken for a waif, Fiona had put on at least thirty pounds since Gracie had last seen her. But the extra weight suited her, sitting well on her frame.

A large gray cat, tucked under her arm, was unperturbed by its owner's enthusiasm. It wasn't bothered by the dogs, either.

Gracie grinned. "I was told someone was going to meet us here, but not who. Not you!"

"So you are back in Tyler!" Fiona exclaimed. "I heard someone say that the other day. Elise Fairmont, at the library, as a matter of fact. She said you'd called in to volunteer."

"I've been back two months, actually. But I was busy settling in and also helping arrange a dog show out at Timberlake Lodge. I didn't have much time for visiting."

"You were at the dog show?" Fiona asked, frowning.

Before Gracie could answer, the assistant manager of the retirement home arrived to collect them.

"Everyone is assembled in the activity room," he said smoothly, glancing at the animals but refraining from making any gesture of friendliness.

Fiona grimaced behind the assistant manager's back as he led them down the hall. Her thoughts mirrored Gracie's: some people loved animals, some people didn't...but those who didn't missed out on so much.

As they neared the door to the activity room, Fiona murmured, "Do you have anything planned for after you leave here?"

"Not a thing," Gracie replied.

"Then let's go have coffee or something and catch up, okay?"

Gracie nodded eagerly.

THE VISIT to Worthington House brought both joy and pain to Gracie's heart, just as her training manual had warned. It was wonderful to see the faces light up with remembered love as the aged men and women responded to the animals who'd come to see them. It was wonderful to hear the stories of the pets they had once shared their lives with. It was sad, though, when it came time to leave and she had to gently disengage Jo-Jo from an octogenarian's reluctant hands, call Jacques away from a game of ball rolling and see the longing for what once had been in numerous pairs of eyes. It was all Gracie could do not to cry.

Fiona patted her shoulder in the parking lot. "It gets to you sometimes," she said. "Especially at first."

"I don't know why. I—" Gracie's throat closed and she was forced to swallow.

"If it's any consolation, it gets easier. You see the real good your pets are doing, and realize that if you and other people like you didn't visit, the residents would be deprived of the experience. And sometimes the animals help people make breakthroughs that traditional medicine can't. I've seen it happen!"

Gracie dabbed at the corner of her eye. "You're probably right."

Fiona grinned. "Of course I'm right. Now, what about that coffee?"

Gracie glanced at the boys and the gray cat—Blossom, she'd learned the cat was named.

"After we drop off the boys, of course," Fiona added. "Did you bring a car?"

"We walked," Gracie answered. "We live only a couple of blocks away."

"Ah, well… I'll tell you what, then. If you don't mind a few dirty dishes—I didn't get a chance to do my tidying up today—we'll go to my house for coffee. Let you see the old neighborhood. There's only one hitch. I have to stop by the clinic where I work. Just for a couple of minutes."

"I don't have anywhere I have to be," Gracie replied.

"Great!" Fiona exclaimed.

The group piled into Fiona's light blue Toyota van. Gracie gave directions and invited her old friend inside her house for a quick tour. Then, minus the poodles, they climbed back into the van and set off for Fiona's workplace.

"My boss is really great about letting me off on Thursday afternoons so I can take Blossom visiting," Fiona said. "He backs Pet Friends one hundred percent."

They traveled down Elm Street, past the square. When they passed the new library Gracie said, "You must not work very far from where you live."

"Only a few blocks," Fiona replied.

The neighborhood grew more and more familiar as they continued on. Gracie had hated the developed area when she and her mother had first moved into it. At nine years old, she hadn't understood why they'd had to leave the farm. Why her father's death and her half brother's marriage had brought about so many changes. At the time, the tensions that existed between Emil and her mother had gone completely over her head. Eventually, though, she'd adjusted to the move, and the little house on Franklin Lane had become home.

"The neighborhood still looks the same," Gracie murmured.

"A lot of new people have moved in over the years."

"Are the people who bought our house still there?"

"It's changed hands three times since you left."

Fiona swung the van into a gravel parking area in front of a two-story, modified Victorian, painted white with forest-green shutters. The narrow porch was open, the floor and steps in forest green as well. A sign hung in the front yard. It said Animal Crackers, along with the clinic's hours of operation.

Gracie stared at it for a long moment before turning to Fiona, who'd already opened the door and hopped out. "This is where you work?" she asked hollowly.

"Yep," Fiona said. "Why don't you come in and see the place? Now that you've moved back to Tyler, you might want to consider changing vets. Dr. Phelps is a very good doctor. Not that Dr. Stewart wasn't. He was great with animals, but not with people. Dr. Phelps is far easier to deal with."

Gracie mumbled something unintelligible.

"Nonsense," Fiona exclaimed, taking it on herself to fill in the blanks. "We won't disturb him! He prob-

ably won't even be here. That's what he does on
Thursday afternoons when I'm out—he makes his
calls in the country.''

How could Gracie continue to refuse? Any more
reluctance and Fiona would start to wonder. She
opened the door and followed her friend up the path
to the porch.

Fiona produced some keys and let them inside. The
familiar smells of a veterinary clinic tickled Gracie's
nose—antiseptics and pet foods and the slightest odor
of dog.

The door opened into a waiting area with molded
plastic chairs, tables scattered with magazines, walls
festooned with posters of dogs and cats and racks offering informative booklets. Fiona slipped behind the
reception desk that curved out from the wall.

''This is it,'' she said. ''My home away from
home. I'll take you in the back rooms in just a minute,
let you look around. But first I have to get that telephone number I forgot. Wade wants me to get a couple of bids on reroofing our house. I keep telling him
that Joe Santori is our best bet, but a driver friend
recommended someone else, and Wade wants me to
at least talk to him.''

She searched the desktop for the piece of paper.

The door to the rear of the clinic opened and Roger
Phelps looked out. ''Fiona?'' he said, ''I heard someone talking and thought I'd better—'' He stopped
abruptly as his gaze locked onto Gracie, who stood
equally transfixed.

''Ah-hah! I found it!'' Fiona cried, clutching the
note. She turned to the doctor, prepared to chatter on,

but upon seeing his arrested state, her gaze followed his to Gracie, who was aware of her old friend's curiosity but unable to do anything about it.

It had been almost a week since they'd last met. Almost a week since she'd walked away from his challenge. In that week Gracie had done her best to forget about him, to wipe him from her memory. Now all it took was a second for her hard work to crumble.

"Grace?" Roger Phelps said.

Her name on his lips made Gracie's body tremble.

"You know each other?" Fiona asked. Then, before either of them could answer, she exclaimed, "Oh, the dog show! You met at the dog show! Why didn't you tell me, Gracie?"

"I didn't know... I didn't..." Her attempts at speech petered out.

Roger moved into the room. As he did, a golden retriever slipped in with him. The dog moved slowly, carefully, acknowledging Fiona with a quick look, but reserving most of her attention for Gracie.

Gracie could see the hesitation as the dog came forward—the short, choppy motion of a limp. The retriever stopped a few feet away from her and waited.

"Serra," Roger murmured.

Serra didn't respond. She continued to look at Gracie, who after a moment slowly lifted her hand, her fingers curled under.

Serra sniffed the back of her hand thoroughly, then turned around and shuffled back to Roger, to sit at his feet. She continued to watch Gracie, but acceptance had replaced suspicion in her eyes.

"Is she a patient?" Gracie asked, her voice strained.

"She was once," Roger said. "This is her home now."

"Did you see that?" Fiona demanded, awe in her tone. "She went right up to her!"

Roger gently smoothed the bright hair on Serra's head and said nothing.

"That's really special, Gracie," Fiona continued. "Serra doesn't usually approach people. She's more apt to hide...like she does from me."

Gracie didn't know what to say. She didn't know what she'd done to merit such behavior.

"You two know each other?" Roger asked, glancing at his assistant.

Fiona nodded. "We're old-time neighbors. Wade and I lived next door to Gracie before she moved to the farm."

"I didn't know that," he said.

Fiona grinned bemusedly. "Was there any reason you should?"

"Ah—no."

"Fiona, maybe we should..." Gracie edged toward the exit.

"Don't you want a quick tour?" Fiona returned. Then, in a conspiratorial aside to Roger, she murmured, "I'm trying to get her to change vets. Look appropriately appealing and professional."

Roger had recovered his aplomb, amusement at the situation seeming to have overcome his moment of shocked surprise. He smiled and managed to look even more handsome in his office, in his element, wearing his white lab coat. "I've been appealing to her for a couple of weeks now, Fiona. She's the one who's resisting. Maybe you can get her to change her mind."

Gracie gave a little gasp.

Never one to be slow on the uptake, Fiona said, "We're not talking about veterinary services, are we?"

"Nope," Roger said, grinning.

Gracie had had enough. She didn't wait for Fiona, but pushed her way through the door and marched out to the van. If she didn't think it would be rude to her friend, she would have started tramping back home. It wasn't that far. *Nothing* was that far in Tyler.

Blossom lifted her head from where she lay curled on the driver's seat, and her huge golden eyes peered at Gracie. The wisdom in those eyes seemed ageless.

"You probably like him, too, don't you?" Gracie snapped, echoing the accusation she'd made to the boys.

Instead of wagging her tail in an attempt to please, as the poodles had done, the cat merely continued to stare at her...as if by some magical, catlike power, she knew that deep down Gracie's protests rang a little hollow.

CHAPTER SEVEN

"I THOUGHT YOU SAID he wasn't going to be there,"
Gracie said as soon as Fiona joined her in the van.

"He usually isn't, but sometimes people cancel appointments. I guess that's what happened today."
Fiona sent her a speculative glance. "Are you completely put off having coffee with me? Do you want
me to take you home?"

Gracie knew that to answer in the affirmative
would only make matters worse. "No," she fibbed.
"I'm not put off."

Fiona couldn't suppress a grin. "You two looked
thunderstruck! I didn't catch on at first, but... I can't
imagine why you're giving him a hard time. If I
weren't married, I know exactly where I'd set my cap.
And I work with the man! I've seen him at his
worst!"

"Fiona!"

Fiona laughed. "All right! All right! I won't say
another word!"

Five minutes later she pulled the van into her driveway, parking it in the shade of a huge old oak. As
Gracie opened her door and stepped out, Fiona collected her cat and started off for her front door.

Gracie followed, but at a slower pace. From this

vantage point, she had a perfect view of the house next door—the house in which she'd grown up. This was the first time she'd seen it since she'd moved away.

Some things about it were different, but the basic structure was still very much the same. It was trimmed in a darker color paint and someone had added a long flower bed across the front. The bushes and trees were a lot larger—those that remained.

Gracie knew every nook and cranny in that house and yard. She knew which floorboards creaked, where the little chips were in the wood frame of the kitchen doorway. She knew about the buildup of paint and putty on the windowsill in her room that her youthful imagination had christened a rearing horse. She remembered the old oak tree in the backyard under which she'd played for hours on end during all but the coldest winter days. As Gracie grew older she'd entertained boys on the front porch and helped her mother make a new seat cover for the wooden swing.

This house was what Gracie thought of when she thought of home, and the poignant memories made her heart contract.

Fiona waited for her on her own porch, the door open in invitation.

"This is the first time I've seen it since I left," Gracie explained as she slipped inside. "Sometimes good memories can hurt almost as much as bad." Then, dipping her chin, she murmured, "I'm sorry, that probably doesn't make a lot of sense."

"It makes perfect sense," Fiona assured her. "I understand completely."

The interior of Fiona's home looked much the same as it always had—warm and welcoming and a bit overcrowded with keepsakes.

"Make yourself at home," Fiona said as she let the cat jump down to the floor. "I'll put the coffee on and be right back."

Blossom paused to touch up her appearance as her owner left for the kitchen, then she hopped up on a windowseat and stared steadily at Gracie.

Gracie took a place on the L-shaped sectional couch and looked back. She liked cats. In their own way, they could be extremely fascinating. But her primary affinity went to dogs, and most cats knew it. She tried to think of something that would break the cat's intense concentration, but nothing worked.

"That's done," Fiona said a moment later, choosing a seat farther along on the couch. When she noticed the slight tension between Gracie and the cat, she shook her head and advised, "Just ignore her. Blossom likes to see if she can intimidate people. It's a game she plays."

"I'm thoroughly intimidated." Gracie laughed.

"Don't let her think she's won."

Gracie made herself relax, not an easy thing to do after the last half hour. First to come upon Roger so unexpectedly, then to see her old home. There were times when she acutely missed her mother, missed being able to talk to her.

"That's better," Fiona approved, aware only of her friend's lessened tension. "So, tell me," she said after a moment. "How has everything been for you? I know you sold the kennel. Was it hard? Do you miss it?''

Gracie answered honestly. ''Yes and no. I miss it, but...''

''But not enough to want it back.''

''No. I was ready to move on. It was time.''

Fiona frowned, obviously sensing that there was more to the story, but not intruding if Gracie didn't want to volunteer any confidences. ''What made you come back to Tyler then, when you had so many other places to choose from? I mean, you're not tied to anything here. You don't have any obligations.''

Gracie had faced that question before. ''I don't know.'' She shrugged. ''I guess since Emil's here, and Sheilie.''

''Are you that close to them? I remember...'' Fiona paused. ''Tell me if I'm butting in where I shouldn't. Wade says it's my worst habit, and he's right.''

''If you hadn't 'butted in' all those years ago, I'm not sure I'd have made it through Mom's illness.''

''I didn't do all that much.''

''I was there, Fiona. You did.''

''*Pffft!*'' Fiona dismissed the notion.

Gracie answered her earlier question. ''Sheilie and I are closer now. Ever since Emil... You know he went through a terrible period after Myrna died.''

Fiona nodded. ''I remember when he fell through the ice on Timber Lake.''

''Oh, he fell, all right. Then instead of trying to float for as long as he could, the man actually dove after his false teeth! Did you know that?''

Fiona chortled. ''I'd heard something like that.''

"If Douglas hadn't been there to go in after him…" Gracie shivered.

Fiona asked perceptively, "Is that when you decided to sell the kennel and move back to town?"

"About then, yes. I—I realized a lot of things about that time. And knew I had to make some changes." She could tell Fiona about Paul and would never have to worry that she would hear about it later from another source. But talking about him now seemed too much of a complication.

"How long are you going to stay?" Fiona asked.

"The lease on my house is for a year."

"Then what?"

"I don't know."

Fiona left to get the coffee and returned with two steaming mugs. She handed one to Gracie, who she had remembered drank it black, then sat back to sip her own, lightened with milk.

"How's Wade?" Gracie asked. Wade Evans had always reminded her of a Great Dane—huge in body, gentle in spirit.

"He's fine," Fiona said, smiling fondly. "He's on his regular run out to the West Coast. I heard from him a couple of days ago. He was held up by an early snowstorm in the Sierra and was waiting it out at a truck stop on the Nevada border." She chuckled. "Some hardship. He usually stops there to shower and eat, and to fritter away a few dollars in the slot machines."

"Does he ever win?" Gracie asked.

"Occasionally. Last trip, he brought me a beautiful pair of candlesticks that he bought in San Francisco with his winnings." Fiona motioned to a pair of ornate brass candlesticks on either end of a cherry sideboard.

"Does he still bring you presents from every trip?"

"Every time. Sometimes it's just a card or a pressed flower he picked from the side of the road, but they mean as much to me as something expensive."

The depth of Fiona's love for her husband, and his for her, gave Gracie's heart another pang. Once, she'd thought she and Paul had that kind of relationship. Even though his base of operations was in Oregon and hers was in Wisconsin, they'd made the most of the times they'd had together at various dog shows across the country. They'd met other times as well, whenever their busy schedules allowed. For six years they'd been together, then…

"The only other person I know who has that same mix of strength and sentiment is Dr. Phelps."

Fiona's words finally got through Gracie's distraction.

"I know you don't want to hear this," Fiona continued, "but it's the truth. They're both so totally male, yet they have a tender core. You should see Dr. Phelps with a hurt animal, Gracie. It's like he shifts into another world where he can communicate with them. He touches them and they grow quiet, as if they know he's going to do his best to make them feel better. I've seen him save animals that other vets would give up on. Serra was one. You saw how she limped? She was in terrible condition when she was brought in last January. She'd been so badly abused.

But he stayed with her, night and day, until she passed the crisis. It's no wonder she's devoted to him.''

"I'm sure he's a good vet," Gracie murmured. Hadn't she said something like that to him?

"Oh, he's more than that!" Fiona replied. "He knows how they *feel!* And that's very important when a patient can't tell you where it hurts or why they're worried or afraid. He senses it."

"Does Wade have reason to be jealous, Fiona?" Gracie teased in self-defense.

Fiona wasn't discouraged. "If I were a different type of woman, he might. And if Dr. Phelps were a different kind of man. I told you earlier that I'd set my cap at him if I could. He's handsome, he has a good character, he—"

"But he's only twenty-eight!" Gracie blurted.

"Ah, so that's it. Age is only a frame of mind, Gracie.''

"It's a darned sight more than that! It's how long you've been in the world, what you've learned along the way, what you've experienced! When he was born, Neil Armstrong was setting foot on the moon! When *I* was born, there wasn't even such a thing as a man-made satellite! That's a lot of difference!''

Fiona started to laugh. "Oh, Gracie!" she gulped when she could finally speak. "You're priceless. Absolutely priceless!"

"Well, it's the truth," she said stoutly.

Fiona set her nearly empty cup on the occasional table in order to wipe her eyes. When she finished she met Gracie's wounded gaze, and her smile faded. "Oh, honey," she said contritely, "I didn't mean to hurt you. It's just…what difference does it make if one person's a few years older than another? Does it mean you can't get along? That you can't fall in love?''

"I never said anything about love!"

Fiona backed off. ''Just don't let what other people think keep you from doing what your heart tells you is right. In the end, you'll be glad you didn't. If Wade and I had paid attention to what the busybodies had to say about our marriage, we'd have separated years ago. I trust Wade to be as faithful to me on the road as if he were a dentist going to work every day in the next town. I'm happy for him that he's doing something he finds rewarding. I'm also happy for myself, because I need a little bit of room in my life, and when he's gone, I get it. We're a perfect match! But the busybodies had a field day until they found out we didn't care what they thought.''

Gracie walked stiffly to the window. Blossom, now asleep, didn't stir.

"This isn't like that," she insisted. ''Roger Phelps and I aren't…'' She shrugged.

Fiona came to stand beside her. The understanding in her expression further tightened Gracie's throat.

"Maybe I'm reading more into this than what there truly is. That's another bad habit I have. It was just the way you two looked, then the way you acted—''

"I didn't act—''

"Just don't close any doors, that's all," Fiona interrupted. "And for goodness sake, don't lock them. Keep your options open, Gracie. You might never know when you'll want to use one.''

Gracie laughed lightly. "That's good advice at any time."

"Of course it is," Fiona said. Then she added, grinning mischievously, "Give the guy a chance!"

The cat awoke and arching her back, stretched hugely. Then she looked at them and started to purr.

"Someone wants attention," Fiona murmured.

Blossom headed straight for Gracie. She slipped her soft gray back beneath Gracie's hand, then made the trip around again, encouraging Gracie to pet her.

"You're very popular today," Fiona said. "First Serra, now Blossom."

"I don't know why," Gracie said softly, continuing to stroke the cat.

"Animals listen to their instincts," Fiona replied.

The double message was clear.

ROGER PEELED OFF the gown and gloves he'd worn to perform surgery. The dalmatian he'd just opened up, in order to retrieve a collection of coins from her tummy, was being attended to by Fiona. She was tracking the patient's progress. The dog lay flat on a rubber mat, her stomach painted with the usual reddish orange, antibacterial goo, her incision held together by a series of neatly tied stitches, a trachea tube still in place.

"Poor girl," Fiona crooned to the still form. "All you wanted to do was go shopping...and since you didn't have any pockets and couldn't carry a purse, you did the only thing you could."

Roger laughed. "You think that's what it was?" he asked.

"Well, yes," Fiona replied. "A girl always wants to look her best, even if she is a bitch."

Roger shook his head at his assistant's play on words. "She wasn't going to get very much with eighty-five cents!" He fingered the three quarters and two nickels that had refused to pass through the dog's digestive track and instead decided to hang around and cause trouble.

"She didn't know that." Fiona smoothed a finger along the dalmatian's cheek. "Poor baby. Next time," she advised, leaning close to stage whisper in the dog's ear, "look for a bill with Ben Franklin's face on it."

"She could get quite an outfit for a hundred dollars," Roger said with a chuckle as he washed his hands.

"Two or three if she went to a discount store."

Roger came back to check the dog's progress, saw that her breathing was good, removed the tube, then helped move her to a waiting cage where she could sleep off the remaining anesthesia.

"I'll call the owner," he said. "Let her know how the operation went."

A few minutes later, after making the call to a very relieved owner, he went to check on a puppy that had been brought to the clinic the day before. The owner of this pup didn't want it, after finding out that it had an inherited eye condition that would require future care. The puppy had been a surprise gift for the owner's son, and the man hadn't wanted it from the beginning. The pup's medical problem seemed to be the excuse he'd been looking for to wiggle free of responsibility.

A casual look at the puppy revealed nothing wrong. He was a typical, playful, five-month-old blond cocker spaniel. It was only upon examining him with a scope that the beginning stages of his juvenile cataracts could be detected.

Roger opened the cage door and took the young dog to the run set up in the side yard, where the clinic's patients could get some exercise.

"What are we going to do with you, boy?" he asked as the pup ran from one fallen leaf to another to busily sniff and mark them. "Who can we find to give you a new home?"

He brought the dog back inside a short time later and again checked on the dalmatian. She was fully conscious now and tried to lift her head to look about.

"It's okay, girl," he said soothingly. "You'll feel better soon."

The dalmatian's head dropped back to the clean towel, Roger's voice seemingly reassuring her.

"How's she doing?" Fiona asked, coming closer.

"In a couple of days she won't remember a thing that happened."

Fiona waggled a small plastic envelope containing the washed coins. "I thought we'd give Mrs. Stevens her change back."

"Staple it to her bill. She might want to frame it."

Fiona chuckled. She started to turn away, then swung back, her gaze curious. "You haven't asked me about Gracie yet. Was I mistaken in what I saw yesterday?"

Roger paused in jotting down notations on the dalmatian's chart. "You don't usually need prompting."

"Gracie Lawson is a friend of mine."

"What does that mean?"

"It means...I don't want to see her get hurt."

Roger finished his notes before giving his assistant his full attention. "In order to get hurt," he said carefully, "a person needs to feel something. Do you think she does?"

Fiona smiled. "I think so. But Gracie's hard to read. She keeps her emotions to herself. That's the way she's always been. I, of course, did as you asked and told her what a great guy you are."

"Did she believe you?"

"Do you want the truth or halfhearted evasion?"

The telephone rang, signaling the end of their midday break. It was two o'clock, time again to open the office to scheduled patients. Fiona hurried to the phone, after which she went to unlatch the front door. Within ten minutes the reception area was populated by two dogs, a cat and a fluffed up, sickly-looking bird.

GRACIE HAD JUST settled in for an evening of watching TV when the doorbell rang. Jacques and Jo-Jo, both cuddled contentedly against her, one on each side, lifted their heads in curiosity.

Gracie, too, was curious. She wasn't expecting anyone. She'd talked to Sheilie earlier in the day and knew that her niece was planning a quiet evening at home with Douglas. She'd even talked with Emil and listened to his plans for readying his ice-fishing equipment for this winter's continuing competition with his neighbor, Gus Lemke. So whoever was calling had to be a friend or an acquaintance or someone selling door-to-door. Or a certain veterinarian.

She switched on the porch light, cracked open the door and peeked outside.

"Hello, Grace," he said, smiling.

Gracie's first instinct was to shut the door, a feeling he must have sensed because he lifted something for her inspection.

"I come bearing a gift," he said. "Or rather, a temporary gift."

Gracie's hesitation was her undoing, because the object he held out to her was a cocker spaniel pup, all wiggly and whimpery from excitement.

Jacques and Jo-Jo stood at her feet, and their tails immediately started to wag.

Gracie let the door swing all the way open as she reached out to take the young pup. The puppy instantly responded to her, straining to reach her face with his tongue.

Jacques and Jo-Jo danced around her feet, demanding a closer look. Jo-Jo gave a happy bark.

Gracie looked from the adorable little dog to Roger. "Who—why?" she stammered.

Roger divested himself of his leather jacket as he stepped into the house. He folded the jacket over the top rail of a straight-back chair. "He's a waif someone left at the clinic."

A soft pink tongue made contact with Gracie's face.

"But why would anyone..." She dissolved into

pleased laughter at the volley of rapid-fire licks that followed.

Two sets of poodle claws dug into her jeans, Jacques adding his barked demand to his son's.

"All right. All right," she told them. "Let's go to the living room." Then, with more circumspection, she added to Roger, "You, too, if you want."

"I'd love to come into your living room," Roger said with a teasing smile.

Gracie held his gaze for a second. He was standing there, all young and virile and very, very handsome. It just wasn't fair!

Gracie sat down with the pup on her lap, allowing the boys access without taking the chance of them overwhelming the younger dog. The pup's tail wagged just as fiercely as theirs did and he gave little grunts of joy. Even though the cocker pup was young, he was almost as large as the mature poodles.

"How old is he?" she asked, looking up.

"Five months, according to his records."

"What happened? Why's he a waif?"

"The owner didn't want him anymore."

She looked down at the pup and straightened his long curling ears. "Didn't want him? Why not? He's adorable. He—"

"He's developing juvenile cataracts."

Gracie's hand stilled. Then she lifted the pup's muzzle and gazed into his dark brown eyes. The little dog's tongue flicked in and out. He thought she wanted more kisses.

Gracie couldn't see it, but she supposed Roger had detected it using a scope. Later on, the telltale clouding of the lenses, which if left uncorrected would eventually leave the little dog blind, would be evident for all to see.

"The owner considered him a faulty product," Roger said.

"That's terrible!" Gracie exclaimed.

"I've seen worse." Roger shrugged. "At least this owner left him with me, and not out on some lonely road to fend for himself."

"What are you going to do?" she asked, instinctively hugging the puppy to her breast.

"Find him a good home, which is why I'm here. I wondered if you'd be willing to take care of him until I find someone willing to adopt him. Someone able to see this thing through."

"An operation," Gracie supplied.

"If he's a candidate. He'll have to go to a specialist and the decision will be made from there." He paused. "What he needs now is a loving place to stay while I look for something permanent, and I couldn't think of anywhere better than here."

"I'm surprised you'd trust me with a pet rat! Being that you think I—"

"Drop it, Grace. That was all a misunderstanding. You know I never felt that way."

Gracie looked down at the little blond dog, who had wiggled free of her hold and was on the floor sniffing a trail to the boys' food and water bowls. Roger Phelps hadn't said it—he hadn't even hinted— but the early onset of cataracts was one of the genetic disorders brought about by a troubled breeding program. It showed a hereditary weakness in which both parents, each very likely from the same family, had passed on the defective gene.

Gracie studied Roger's face, trying to gauge if he was interested in making a point, or if he was sincere.

"All right," she said after a moment, "I'll keep him for however long it takes. What's his name?"

"He doesn't have one, as far as I know. The owner refused to say."

"What about 'Peter'?" she suggested.

"Peter he is," Roger decreed. Then, leaning back, he spread his arms along the back of the couch and, oozing sophistication and confidence, said, "I could sure use a cup of coffee and some sparkling conversation. How do you feel about providing both?"

Gracie had the distinct impression that it would take a dynamite charge to get him up off that couch. Particularly after Jacques—traitor that he was— hopped up beside him and made himself comfortable against Roger's thigh.

CHAPTER EIGHT

"THERE'S NO WAY I can guarantee *sparkling* conversation," Gracie said. "Will ordinary conversation do?"

"It sounds wonderful," Roger agreed.

Gracie went into the kitchen and started the automatic coffee maker, then she searched in her pantry for something to serve with it. She'd been planning to go to the grocery store tomorrow, so her supplies were low. She found the remains of several different kinds of cookies and arranged them on a plate, which she carried into the living room when the coffee was done.

He wasn't seated where she'd left him. He'd gotten up to study the photographs clustered on a glass-topped table. Most were likenesses of her family— her mother, Emil, Sheila as a child. A few were of friends from across the country, mostly taken at dog shows. Another was of her and Hortense, just after they'd won Best in Show at a competition in St. Louis.

It was that photo he'd lifted to study. "When was this taken?" he asked.

"About five years ago. That's Hortense, Jo-Jo's mother."

"She died, I understand."

"Yes."

She placed the tray on the coffee table, and he came back to the couch to accept his cup. He sat back without adding sugar or cream, taking it just as she did.

All the while the young cocker was busily checking out the room, with Jo-Jo right behind him. Occasionally the pup would roll over and wave his paws in the air, then he'd hop up and resume making discoveries.

"Don't worry," Roger said. "He's housebroken."

"I wasn't worried," Gracie replied.

A little silence stretched between them. Gracie was very aware of him, aware that this was their first conventional contact. A man, a woman—talking. She searched for something to say.

"Why did you leave Tyler all those years ago?" Roger asked, taking the onus off her, but introducing a subject that made her frown. "Or isn't that 'ordinary' enough?" he teased. Yet his teasing contained a serious edge.

Gracie's grip tightened on her cup. Was this a part of his determination to 'get to know her'? "I wanted to see if I could run a business myself."

"What made you choose a breeding kennel?"

"Why not?" she replied lightly.

"Most of the time, people have a reason for what they do."

"Why did you leave medical school?" she countered.

"Because I hated it. Because it wasn't my idea, it was my father's."

"Did you always do what your father wanted?"

Roger smiled slowly. "I asked you first."

Gracie took a perfunctory sip of her coffee, then settled the cup and saucer back on the low table. "I couldn't find anything else I wanted to do. Office work bored me, I didn't like sales clerking. I groomed dogs for a time, enjoyed it, talked to people who bred them, then decided I could do it, too."

"And Grace Farms was the result."

She nodded.

"Why'd you sell it?" he asked, still probing for a hidden truth. "From everything I heard, it was highly respected by your peers. Did you get bored with it, too? Or discover that you didn't really like it? I wouldn't have thought, with it being so successful, that would be the case. A big-time breeder has to be pretty devoted. So there must be some other—"

"What have you heard?" she challenged, her back stiffening.

"I try not to listen to rumors. I know firsthand how they can hurt." He gave a disarming smile. "I suppose you heard about my family's scandal? Even in the country?"

"I heard…something."

"I was at school in New York. That's when I asked myself why should I be doing something I didn't want to do, when my father… That's when I quit." He paused. "I suppose, now, that looks rather juvenile."

"Do you ever regret doing it?" she asked, curious in spite of herself.

"I'd regret even more not being a vet. I love it. It's my calling."

"I loved my dogs," Gracie said. "All my dogs. Leaving them was one of the hardest things I've ever had to do."

"Then why—?"

Gracie stood up. She didn't want to be rude, but this tête-à-tête hadn't been her idea in the first place. "I was planning an early night tonight. So if you don't mind…"

Roger cocked his head. "Is that a hint that I've overstayed my welcome?" He set his cup on the table next to hers and slowly unfolded his length from the couch.

She edged away, not wanting to chance contact.

He seemed to pick up on her motivation, and lifting an eyebrow, smiled at her. "I've told you before, I don't bite."

Foolishly, regardless of her efforts not to, Gracie blushed.

Jacques looked up from his sleep on the couch. Jo-Jo and Peter had stretched out on the floor nearby, the pup having finally exhausted himself.

"Looks like they get along just fine," he said, chucking Jacques under the chin. "I enjoyed the coffee and conversation, Grace. Thank you. And thank you for agreeing to take Peter. I'll look back in on you tomorrow, to see how things are progressing. In the meantime…" He reached out and cupped the back of her neck before she could move away. "This is something I just have to do…"

His brown eyes roamed over her face, twinkling

with good humor as he pulled her closer. Then his mouth fastened onto hers.

Gracie stood frozen in place. She hadn't expected... The warmth of his lips broke through her frozen state. They moved, they cajoled, they took what she wouldn't give freely, until she began to respond.

As had happened before, all barriers shattered. Her lips parted, grew eager. She was consumed with a searing need to get closer, to move further, but above all, to continue this intoxicating pleasure. It had been so long....

After endless, breathless moments she broke away, untangling herself from his continuing insistence, freeing herself from the hard outline of his body.

Good humor no longer had a place in his gaze as he looked down at her, only desire.

A pulse hammered at the base of Gracie's throat. She tried to draw a breath. She hadn't meant...

Slowly he straightened, gaining control. A fleeting smile touched his lips. "Lovely Grace," he said softly, as he had once before. Then he went to the door, shouldered his way back into his leather jacket and slipped outside.

Gracie remained motionless.

She hadn't meant that to happen!

Why had it happened?

Was she that lonely? That love-starved?

She made a small sound and turned out the light. For a long time afterward she sat in the darkened room, staring at nothing.

ROGER LAY IN BED with his right arm hanging off the side, his fingertips curled on the rug. Serra, lying nearby, stirred until her muzzle touched his hand. A soft puff of warm air played over his skin each time she exhaled.

When she'd first started to sleep in his room at night he'd offered to share his bed with her, but she'd steadfastly refused, preferring a place on the floor instead. She hadn't rejected all contact, though. An occasional light touch provided contentment.

Roger smiled to himself.

He'd won the heart of one fair lady. Could he possibly hope for two?

Gracie. Grace... His body responded at the mere thought of her name.

The telephone rang and Roger groaned. He hoped it wasn't another emergency call. Between lying awake long hours at night thinking about Gracie and having to go out on emergencies, he was getting precious little sleep. He checked his watch as he reached for the phone. It was only twelve-thirty.

"Animal Crackers," he mumbled into the receiver.

"That is the most ridiculous name!" a woman's light voice complained.

"Missy?" Roger pushed up to a sitting position, instantly concerned. He checked his watch again. The hands still read twelve-thirty. "What's up? Is anything wrong?"

His sister's laugh was brittle. "Oh, no, nothing's wrong! Only my marriage is about to disintegrate, that's all. But then, since that kind of thing already runs in the family, it's not all that unexpected. John and I...we—'' Tears closed her throat and she dissolved into racking sobs.

Roger adjusted his grip on the receiver. ''Missy,'' he said after a moment. ''Missy, get a hold. I can't help if you don't tell me what—''

''He thinks I'm wrong to keep Dad and the boys apart. All along he didn't say anything. I thought he agreed with what I was doing. He knows why! He knows the way I feel! But tonight—out of the blue, or at least what I thought was out of the blue—he told me I'm hurting the boys. Me! Hurt my boys! As if I'd ever—!'' She took a shaking breath. ''You know what's happened, don't you? Dad talked to John. He went around my back and talked to my husband. Of all the—! I can't believe he'd do that! I can't—!''

Roger thought it was time to interrupt. ''That doesn't sound like something Dad would do, Missy. Are you sure?''

''Of course I'm sure! The way John talked, the words he used...it was Dad all over!''

''That doesn't mean—''

''Ask him! Ask Dad for me, Roger. See what he says. And if he admits it, get him to make everything right again. It's the least he can do, after...'' She started to sob again.

Roger let her cry. When his sister was this upset there was little use trying to reason with her. Five minutes of tears, sniffs and gulps later, Melissa became calmer.

''That's better,'' Roger soothed. He tried to relieve her distress by saying the words calmly, as he would to one of his patients. Melissa was reacting just as blindly as a hurt animal to the pain.

"If you weren't there to help me, Roger, I don't know what I'd do. Promise me you'll talk to him. Please?"

"I'll talk to him. I'll talk to him tomorrow. But you need to talk to John, too. Calmly, quietly—"

"He's *so* unreasonable!"

"Did you hear what I said? Calmly, quietly, without accusations."

"You think I'm acting like a baby, don't you?" She sniffed, starting to sound aggrieved with him, too. "Tell the truth."

Roger heaved a long sigh. "I think you need to do some belated growing up, Missy."

The answer didn't please her. "You're just as bad as he is. Cut from the same cloth. Mom said that about you, did you know that? And she was right! I can't imagine what I thought I was doing when I called to ask you for help. You're on his side!"

"I'm not on anyone's side, Missy, with the exception of your boys. None of this is their fault."

"Like it is mine. Go on! Say it! Oh, *men!* You'll stick together no matter what!"

"Missy…" He tried again to soothe her.

"Why don't you go take a flying leap!" she shouted and slammed the phone down so hard that the clatter traveled up the line from Chicago to Tyler and made Roger jerk the receiver away from his ear.

Serra had gotten up to check on him. She'd heard the tension in his voice and, sensing that something was wrong, balanced her front paws on the mattress and nudged him with her nose.

Roger hung up the phone and rubbed her golden head. "There's nothing you can do anything about, girl," he said. "And darned little that I can, either."

The phone rang again and Roger looked at it. He didn't want to pick it up. But duty asserted itself— duty to his sister and to his patients. He answered the call, and this time it was an animal emergency, something that he could attempt to solve. He threw back the covers, dressed, patted Serra on the head and hurried down the stairs to the waiting van.

GRACIE ENJOYED having the cocker puppy as a guest. His playful exuberance was hard to resist. Life was a wonderful game to him, and he threw all his energy into everything he did, so much so that sleep would sometimes overtake him.

Gracie had just bounced the soft rubber ball across the floor for the umpteenth time in a row when suddenly Peter plopped down and went to sleep.

"Well!" Gracie chuckled, as Jacques and Jo-Jo looked on. She could have sworn that they chuckled, too.

She'd just gone over to the window to retrieve the ball herself when a car pulled into her driveway, one that she'd never seen before. It was a dark blue Saturn.

As she continued to look at it, Roger Phelps stepped out, and immediately her heart rate started to gallop. *Stop it!* she scolded herself. *There's nothing between you. Nothing! The kiss was just a kiss—both of them!*

She hurried to the door with the idea of intercepting him. She didn't want him inside her house again. He unnerved her, made her react in inexplicable ways.

When he saw her standing in the doorway, he flashed a smile. "You've come to meet me," he said. "Do I take that as a good sign, or has Peter done something I'll have to apologize for?"

Gracie hadn't thought he'd take it like that, as if she were hurrying to meet him! She scrambled for an excuse. "I was just coming to collect the mail. I—I didn't know you were even here." To prove her point she reached into the metal box beside the door, only to come up with nothing. "That's strange. I thought I heard the mailman."

"So I have nothing to apologize for?" he asked.

That depended entirely upon your point of view, Gracie thought. She figured that he did, for taking advantage of her vulnerable state last night. But she doubted that he'd agree.

He didn't stop at the threshold. Once again, he came inside as if he belonged there. While he waited for her to close the door, she felt his eyes linger on her.

"As you can see," she said, trying to pretend that this was purely a business call, "Peter's not a bother."

Roger took in the state of all three dogs. "Looks like they're all played out," he said. "Have they been keeping you busy?"

"Well, Jacques hasn't so much."

Roger's golden brown eyes came to rest again on her. Gracie tried not to notice how handsome he looked in his tan slacks and cream pullover sweater, which was worn on top of a rust-colored shirt.

"I've got some good news," he said. "I've found Peter a home."

"Already?" Gracie blinked, surprised.

Roger nodded. "I had an emergency call last night, out at Britt Marshack's farm. One of the goats that helped start her yogurt business went down. It looked worse than it was, actually. The nanny had eaten something she shouldn't. Anyway, I told Britt about Peter and she wants him."

"She knows about his eyes?" Gracie asked.

"I told her everything."

Gracie looked at the little pup. It hadn't taken long for her to become attached to him. But then, when she was an active breeder she'd only sold dogs to people who she knew would treat them well and take excellent care of them. Each puppy left with a piece of her heart.

"She'll give him a good home," Roger assured her. "You don't have to worry about that."

"I know."

There was a short silence, then he said, "I never thought that you might want him. Especially since—"

"No, you're right. He's a sweet little guy, but the boys are all I should be dealing with right now."

His eyes narrowed. Gracie knew he was close to asking another probing question, and to prevent that she blurted out, "I spent my first years on a farm."

"The farm where your brother lives now?"

"Yes, it was our father's place."

"I envy you. I grew up in Tyler."

"I did, too, after I turned nine."

"Would you believe me if I told you I didn't have a pet until I was an adult?" He smiled at her look of surprise. "It's true. My mother thought pets were too messy."

"Then what made you…"

He shrugged and laughed. "I didn't say I never tried to get one. I was just never allowed to keep it. I'd drag one kind or another home every month or so, everything from turtles to a friend's discarded pet tarantula. Possibly now I'm overcompensating."

"Fiona says you have a special talent with animals."

"Ah, Fiona."

"You're very lucky to have her."

"So she tells me, almost every day."

Gracie looked at Peter again. "Do you want to take him now?"

Roger nodded, then he said, "I have an idea. Why don't you come with us? Having you along might make the transition easier for him."

Gracie started to refuse. The words were on the top of her tongue when she heard herself say instead, "If you think it would help."

Five minutes later, she and Peter were being ushered out of the house and into Roger Phelps's car.

PETER RODE in a carrier tucked securely into position on the back seat. He went to sleep almost immediately, but when he woke up a short time later, Gracie slid her fingers through the wire and tickled the underside of his chin.

"You're going to your new home, Peter," she said softly. "With some very nice people who have enough children to keep you busy." She turned to Roger. "How many children does Britt have?"

"Five. Matt, Christy, David, Renee and Jacob. Jacob's the baby. He's two."

"He's hers with her new husband."

"Jake Marshack," Roger confirmed, glancing away from the road. "Have you met him yet?"

Gracie shook her head.

"He's a nice guy," Roger said. "He quit his job with a dairy company to help Britt run the yogurt business. Although in this case, it was probably more like being stampeded. Yes! Yogurt was a huge success before Britt was fully prepared for it. Jake was almost forced to help out."

"Do you know? The other day I saw an ad for Yes! Yogurt in *People*."

"It's a Cinderella story. I wasn't in Tyler when Britt went through her bad times, but I've been told she almost lost her farm."

"I heard that, too," Gracie said. "Were you in school in New York? Or had you already left?"

Roger laughed. "A little of both. I think it was all happening about the same time."

What am I doing? one part of Gracie's mind demanded. Why am I encouraging him like this? She knew where it would lead...was that what she wanted? But she *wasn't* encouraging him, another part of her defended. She was only being friendly. Wasn't she?

"Are you and your father... Have the two of you... made up?" she asked.

"We've come to terms," Roger replied. "He's changed, I've changed. I've learned a lot about tolerance and compassion in the past four or five years."

Gracie thought about Dr. George Phelps. He'd always been an imposing figure in the day-to-day life of Tyler. He'd had the power of money and influence, almost as much as the Ingalls family.

She said, "When you talk about tolerance and compassion, do you feel it for people like Peter's previous owner?"

"I suppose I do. Peter was a gift. Whoever gave him to the man's son didn't check to see if a puppy would be a welcome addition to the household."

"But to reject him because he wasn't perfect! If it was money for the operation, I could understand. Something could have been worked out, though, couldn't it?"

"Probably, but it wasn't that. I asked. No, Peter will be far better off in a home where he's wanted."

"You do this a lot, don't you?" she asked, already sure of his answer.

"Seems to be part of the job description. The only pet I never found a home for was Serra. And I didn't, I think, because I didn't really want to give her away. I wanted her myself."

"Fiona told me how she almost died, how you pulled her through."

"All I did was help out here and there. It was Serra's pluck and determination that won the day."

"Did you ever find out who abused her?"

"It was a drifter passing through. I saw them out on the highway a few days before Serra was found so badly injured. I blame myself for not doing something, but there wasn't any reason to intervene—then. You can't just take an animal away from a person because he looks unsavory. Some of those drifters would give their last bite of food to their pet, the pet means that much to them. This one…" His lips thinned even now. "This one was different."

Gracie got the idea that that particular drifter had better not drift through Tyler or its environs ever again. Not as long as Roger drew breath.

"She doesn't trust people anymore," Roger said after a few moments had passed. "She shies away. It upsets Fiona that she can't make friends with her. That's why it was so unusual that she went to you."

"I can't imagine why she did," Gracie said.

"Maybe she sees the same thing in you that I do— that you're someone very special."

"Roger," she protested, "this has to stop. Like I said the first day I met you—"

A car, a silver Buick, tore around the curve ahead, and instead of keeping to its lane on the narrow highway, headed straight toward them.

Roger reacted instantly, leaning on the horn and the brakes, and in a few seconds—just feet from impact— the car swerved back into its lane. Gravel and dirt flew in the air as the driver overcompensated and the speeding car's tires slid onto the shoulder before it was righted again.

As the car whizzed past, Gracie recognized the driver—Angus Watson! Instinctively, she gasped.

Roger misread the reason for her reaction. As soon as he could he pulled over to the side of the road and turned to take her by the shoulders. "Are you hurt?" he asked worriedly. "Did you hit your head? Did the seat belt—"

Gracie knew her face had whitened, both from the scare and from the shock of recognition. She hadn't seen Angus Watson since learning who he was. "I— I'm fine," she stammered. "I'm not hurt. It's just…" She stopped. She couldn't explain to Roger or to anyone who Angus Watson was! Or why seeing the man had so unnerved her. She had promised Brick.

She bit her bottom lip, and Roger's expression tightened. Almost as if he couldn't stop himself, he pulled her head against his chest and held it there.

Gracie knew that she should draw away, but the refuge he offered was hard to refuse. She stayed where she was, breathing his masculine scent, feeling his warmth, absorbing his strength.

"I'm sorry," she apologized after a moment, pulling back.

He wouldn't release her fully. He lifted a hand to brush the flyaway hairs from her face. His touch was gentle, caring.

"I thought we were goners for a second there," he said huskily. "If it had happened, I can't think of anyone I'd rather—"

Gracie couldn't bear to hear it. "No!" she said, breaking his hold. She moved away with a little twist.

Several seconds passed. "Who's Paul, Grace?" Roger asked. "What does he have to do with your selling your breeding program? Why were people at the dog show whispering about him and you?"

Gracie's blood ran cold. She hadn't realized that people would think… Was that the story that would eventually get back to Paul and Jessica? That she remained so crushed she'd had to get out of the business?

Gracie shook her head, denying it. It wasn't like that! It wasn't—

Roger pulled her back against him. "It doesn't matter to me," he said. "But it seems to matter to you. All I want—"

Gracie struggled to get away again, not from him but from what people thought. "It's not like that!" she cried. "I sold the kennel because I wanted to. It didn't have anything to do with Paul. Grace Farms had taken over my life. Each day, every day, all I thought about was…"

She broke off at the realization that maybe Paul did have something to do with her decision to sell, after all. Not in the way everyone thought, but because she had pulled in so far in order not to be hurt again that she had closed herself off to life.

All the fight suddenly left her. She slumped in her seat, her heart beating fast as she tried to rein in her speeding thoughts.

She could feel Roger continuing to look at her, but she couldn't look back. Then she remembered Peter.

How had he fared in the near-accident? She jerked to her knees to check and found him perfectly safe in his carrier.

"He's fine," she said shakily, settling back. As if Roger couldn't see for himself. She was ashamed of her behavior. Ashamed that he had been there to witness it. "That was a close call, wasn't it?" she asked, laughing without meaning to. "These farm roads can be really dangerous, they're so narrow. All it takes is one driver not paying attention. There were always accidents on the road in front of Grace Farms. Some of us petitioned the state to have it widened, but they didn't do it. At least, not before I left." She babbled on, sounding for all the world like a demented parrot.

Roger restarted the engine and pulled back onto the roadway. He was silent as the car accelerated.

Gracie looked miserably out the window. Why did it matter to her that she had shown him a part of herself that she wasn't proud of? Had spoken of a time and a person she had discussed with no one before? Roger Phelps wasn't anything to her. What he thought, what he felt didn't matter. Did it?

CHAPTER NINE

THEIR VISIT to Britt Marshack's farm proved more enjoyable than Gracie had thought possible. Roger had come back to life shortly after turning into the farm's driveway. He had bantered jovially with Britt and her husband, Jake, and teased the younger children when he handed over Peter. He'd even been friendly to her, if a little reserved.

The puppy took to the Marshacks as he had taken to Gracie. Home was where he was, and where people gave him attention and fed him. As time went by and he grew older, his loyalties would focus and he would become a part of the family, just as were the older dog, Daffy, a yellow female Lab, the three black-and-white cats, and the previous most recent addition to the menagerie, a young black dog of indeterminate parentage—all brought together by the children for a formal introduction.

"Can he be mine for my birthday?" the youngest daughter, Renee, asked. At almost eleven, she was a chubby younger version of her mother, with the same curly, red-gold hair and blue-gray eyes. "Please, Mommy, please? I'll take good care of him, not like those other people who had him." She scooped the cocker pup into her arms and hugged him close. "I won't ask for anything else. And you let Christy have a puppy when Tex had her litter!''

"When's your birthday?" Gracie asked.

"On Sunday," Renee answered. "Tomorrow."

Britt smiled and looked at her husband. "Well, why not?" she said.

Jake nodded his agreement.

Renee let out a little squeal and hurried over to her brother.

David grinned. "Maybe we can teach him to be a good guard dog. Not like Daffy. She even likes that man next door."

"Daffy likes everybody."

"Yeah, when he yelled at her, she kept wagging her tail."

"Man next door?" Roger asked.

Britt's face lost some of its natural warmth. "Angus Watson," she said. "He's renting Judy Lowery's old place."

"He doesn't happen to drive a silver Buick, does he?" Roger asked.

"I think he does," she said. "Why?"

"He almost ran us off the road earlier. Man drives like a maniac."

"I wouldn't put anything past him," Britt murmured, then hastily added, "But then I don't really know him. He's only been renting the place for a short time. It's just a feeling I have."

Gracie didn't know Britt Marshack well enough to be sure, but she had the distinct impression Britt knew more about Angus Watson than she was letting on. Judy Lowery was her good friend—the Judy Lowery who was also the missing Daphne Sullivan's half sister. Had Brick talked to Britt about Angus Watson's connection to Celeste Huntington? And about Celeste Huntington's threat?

Gracie volunteered, "I met him when he was staying at Timberlake Lodge, during the dog show. He, ah, he's highly allergic to dogs."

David's youthful laugh trilled. "No wonder he yelled at Daffy, then!" he exclaimed.

ON THE WAY BACK to town Roger again retreated into silence, while Gracie resumed watching the passing countryside. It wasn't an enjoyable exercise.

Finally, he asked, "Did you recognize him earlier?"

"Who?" she said.

"The man in the car. Angus…I forget his last name."

"Watson," she supplied.

He speared her with a look and waited for her to continue.

"Well," she hedged, "I wasn't sure…"

"What is it about this guy?" he demanded. "I distinctly picked up on something from Britt. She doesn't like him, not one little bit. But she says she doesn't know him, that he's lived next door for barely any time at all. That doesn't add up."

"You'd have to ask her," Gracie said.

"Now *you're* doing it!"

"Doing what?" She clung to innocent inquiry.

He tapped his fingers on the steering wheel.

She searched for something that would take his

mind off Angus Watson. "How were you able to do this today? Isn't the clinic open on Saturday?"

"Only until one o'clock," he answered flatly. She hadn't diverted him.

She tried a smile. "I think you found Peter a good home. Little Renee's really taken to him."

"She's a sweet kid. You're not going to tell me, are you?"

"I don't have anything to tell. I don't know him, either."

"Maybe I'll ask around about him," he mused, glancing at her from the corner of his eye. "See if other people—"

"No!" She responded with more urgency than his words warranted and quickly realized her mistake. "I mean...why? It doesn't really matter, does it? So he's not a good driver. Neither are a lot of people."

He lapsed into silence again and Gracie's hands curled into fists. What was happening? How had she managed to get herself to this state? To act so defensive first about Paul, and now Angus Watson.

The answer to Angus Watson was simple. Sheilie had confided in her and Brick had made a request. Aside from that, Gracie didn't know him. Neither did she know Daphne Sullivan. Or Celeste Huntington! Her only concern in the matter was Sheilie's continued safety.

She heaved a sigh and tried to put all of it out of her mind. Maybe Roger would do the same. Maybe she could go on as if this afternoon had never happened.

She was concentrating so hard on clearing her mind

that she wasn't aware when Roger turned into her driveway or that he had cut the engine.

Her first notice came when his warm hand curved over hers. "You're home, Sleeping Beauty," he murmured.

The warmth in his voice unsettled her. She wasn't expecting it. "I wasn't asleep," she denied.

"Grace," he said after a moment, "I want you to come out with me tomorrow night. We'll have dinner at Timberlake Lodge, and I promise I won't ask any questions you don't want to answer."

Gracie instinctively started to shake her head, but he stopped her.

"I'm not going to take no for an answer. I'll keep asking."

She looked at him and she could see that he meant it. "All right," she said at last, "but only if I can pay my own way. We'll go out as friends, nothing more."

If her stipulation had caught him off guard, he didn't show it. "All right," he agreed. "Whatever it takes. I'll pick you up at seven-thirty."

Gracie got out of the car and made her way, alone, up the pathway to her house.

GRACIE COULDN'T SETTLE down the next morning. She went to an early Sunday service, made calls to her group of elders, bathed both poodles. In the afternoon, she paid a visit to Sheila. Douglas was off to a meeting of his history reenactment group, and Sheila welcomed the company.

"I have something to tell you," her niece said conspiratorially when she met her at the door. "The latest about you-know-who and you-know-what."

Gracie followed Sheila into her nicely appointed kitchen and settled in the chair she indicated.

"The last time we talked, Angus Watson was a guest at the hotel, wasn't he?" Sheila asked, as she completed preparation of a casserole. She seemed to have no trouble balancing the demands of her job at the hotel and her recent marriage. In fact, she was thriving.

"He was," Gracie agreed.

"Well, he's not anymore. He's renting a place now. Judy's old farmhouse! Can you believe the man's crust? He's actively hunting for Judy's sister, out to do her no good—at the very least, take her baby away! And he makes the house she last lived in his base of operations. Talk about hiding in plain sight! And another thing. Do you know he spends hours every day in town, talking to people and asking questions? And one of the questions—I was told this by the person he asked—is where people from around here go when they want to take a short vacation. As in 'Where's Daphne'? This person actually likes him! Can you believe it?"

Nothing would surprise Gracie about Angus Watson anymore. "I knew he was at the farm," she said calmly.

"You did?"

"I was at Britt Marshack's yesterday."

"I didn't know you knew Britt all that well."

"I don't. It's a long story. Finish yours first."

Sheila immediately returned to her tale. "He was

sent another fax before he checked out, and I took a copy of it to Brick. This one just told him to 'hurry up with the delivery.' I pushed and Brick told me a little more. He said Britt and her kids were keeping an eye on him at the farm—from afar, of course. He wants to know Angus Watson's comings and goings and what people visit him. It's all being done from the hill above Judy's place. One of the kids has a telescope.''

''I had a feeling Britt knew something,'' Gracie said.

''Why were you out at her farm?'' Sheila asked.

Gracie knew her answer was going to create another storm of questions, but if she was going to go to the lodge that night with Roger, the news would be all over Tyler before they were served dessert. She didn't want Sheila to hear it from someone else.

''I went with Roger Phelps,'' Gracie said. ''He brought a puppy in need of a new home out to Britt.''

Sheila placed a lid on the casserole and slid it into the oven. Then she joined her at the table. ''Tell me all,'' she said. ''This sounds interesting.''

Gracie rolled her eyes. ''It's not, particularly. He needed someone to keep an abandoned puppy for a night or two, so I kept it. Then he found it a home and I went along on the delivery.''

''You make it sound so cut and dried,'' Sheila complained.

''Because it was. The only thing even remotely exciting was when Angus Watson almost crashed into us with his car. That's it.'' Gracie conveniently forgot to mention what had happened after.

"Angus Watson almost hit you?" Sheila echoed.

"Roger got his attention in time and he swerved back out of the way."

"Where did all this happen?" Sheila breathed, her eyes wide.

"Near Britt's farm. When Roger told her about it, Britt said Angus Watson had recently moved in next door."

"Drat the man! I wish he'd go away!"

Gracie had had more than enough of Angus Watson herself. She wished he'd go away, too…for everyone's sake. She took a breath. "Sheilie…" she began.

Sheila feigned concern. "I don't like it when you sound so serious."

"I'm having dinner tonight with Roger Phelps."

"You are?" Her expression instantly brightened.

"We're going out as friends, nothing more. I just wanted you to know, so—"

"I think that's wonderful!" her niece exclaimed.

"Did you hear what I said? Friends…we're going out as friends."

"'From friendship comes the best marriages.' Isn't that a famous old saying?"

"Sheilie!"

Sheila tried to look contrite.

"It's nothing like what you're thinking," Gracie continued. "We're not… Roger and I aren't…"

"Has he kissed you yet?" Sheila asked.

Gracie couldn't prevent a wash of color from staining her cheeks.

Sheila reached for her hand and squeezed it. "Why are you fighting this so hard?" she asked earnestly.

"If you like him and he likes you? I was only teasing about getting married. Just to see how you'd react. What's the harm in going out with him?"

"People will talk," Gracie said.

"What else is new?"

"I'm older than he is."

"So?"

"I'm not ready—" she took a breath "—I'm not ready for another relationship."

"He's not Paul, Aunt Grace."

Gracie's gaze jerked to her niece's, and Sheilie smiled faintly. "I've known about Paul Thorpe for a long time. From before Mom died. Diane Jennings was worried about you, about the way you were reacting. She told me what had happened, hoping I could help. She didn't tell anyone else."

"All this time...you knew?" Gracie murmured.

Sheila nodded.

Gracie pulled her hand free and turned away. She didn't know what she felt, what she thought. It wasn't any of Diane's business to go telling tales! If she'd wanted to hide herself away and never see anyone, that was her choice! Diane shouldn't have... Gracie brushed the hair away from her face. "Why didn't you say anything?" she asked huskily. "Why didn't you tell me you knew?"

"If you'd wanted me to know, you'd have told me yourself, wouldn't you?"

"Still, you never let on..."

"Would it have helped if I did?"

"No."

A small silence stretched between them. Then

Gracie said, "I suppose you heard more talk at the dog show."

"Only a little. Mostly, it was speculation about why you'd sold the kennel."

Gracie looked up. "I didn't sell it to avoid seeing Paul!"

"I didn't think you did."

"Do the gossips in Tyler know about this now?"

"I haven't heard a word. Probably not."

"Diane must have put the fear of God into the local poodle-club members."

"Either that, or they respect you enough themselves not to talk. Most of the people I spoke with were on your side. They thought that what he did to you—the *way* he did it—was rotten. For the record, I do, too!"

Gracie smiled slightly.

Sheila again took her hand. "Are you still in love with him?" she asked quietly.

Gracie shook her head wordlessly.

"Is that why you're so determined to reject Roger? You're afraid of being hurt again? You're not the kind of person who should go through life alone, Aunt Grace. You're warm, you're funny, you're generous. You have a lot to give. And you deserve those same things in return."

"From Roger," Gracie finished for her.

"From Roger or someone else." Sheila hesitated, then asked, "How do you feel about Roger, deep down? Do you like him?"

"I—I don't know," Gracie said tightly.

Sheila's smile was tender. "You're the only aunt I

have, and I'm your only niece. Listen to what I'm going to tell you. Don't leave things too late if you do come to care for him. Our family curse is that we hide from our feelings. Don't let that happen to you.''

As Gracie drove home a short time later she pondered everything that Sheila had said. And she was amazed at how wise her niece had become. It was true. The Lawsons did seem to make a fetish of not displaying their emotions, and in some quarters that could easily be mistaken for not having them. Her father had been what could be termed a hard man, dedicated to working his dairy farm and providing materially for his family. Their home never had been filled with laughter or outward signs of love. Neither, apparently, had the home he'd made with his first wife. That trait had been passed down to Emil, and, it seemed, to herself. Possibly more than she wanted to believe?

ROGER STOPPED OFF at the Tyler Police Substation. He knew most of the staff there through his work with their pets. Brick Bauer's wife, Karen, who was once captain of the force and now was at school studying for her Masters degree in criminology, owned a German Shepherd. Steve Fletcher, a lieutenant, owned a mutt and two cats. Orson Clayton, a sergeant, and his family raised Dutch rabbits. Hedda Rakes, one of the dispatchers, was the proud owner of a cockatiel. Most of the patrol officers had come through his doors as well, with everything ranging from snakes to sheep.

He was hailed by numerous greetings as the shift

changed. These he returned with good humor, but his objective wasn't to exchange pleasantries. He wanted to talk to Brick. Gracie's evasive reaction to his questions about Angus Watson had made Roger curious, especially added to Britt Marshack's odd behavior. Something was going on, something that didn't feel right.

He tapped on the door to the captain's office and received a curt, "In," as permission to enter.

Surprise showed on Brick's face as Roger took a seat on the other side of his desk.

"I'll only take a minute of your time," Roger said. "I want to ask you about someone. A stranger in town. A man named Angus Watson. Do you know anything about him?"

Brick's expression tightened imperceptibly. He folded his arms on his desk. "First, tell me what you think you know."

"I don't know anything. That's why I'm asking you."

"What makes you suspicious of him?" Brick asked flatly in his best police don't-give-away-a-thing manner.

"He's a reckless driver, for one thing. He almost hit me yesterday."

"Are you here to file a complaint?"

Roger knew when he was being stonewalled. "I'm here to find out if there's anything I should be worried about if a friend of mine is acquainted with him."

"What friend?" Brick retorted.

Roger gritted his teeth. "Does it matter?"

"It might."

"Gracie Lawson."

Brick relaxed a bit, enough to give a tight smile. "I don't think you have to worry."

"But someone else might," Roger countered. His bad feeling about Angus Watson was being confirmed.

"I didn't say that."

Roger's eyes narrowed. *No, you don't have to,* he thought, *but I feel it.*

Roger got to his feet and Brick did as well.

"Just do me a favor," Brick said. "Keep what you think to yourself. Don't spread it around."

Brick held out his hand and waited for Roger to take it.

The two men exchanged a sturdy shake. But as Roger left the room, he found himself no more enlightened about Angus Watson than he'd been when he'd entered. The one good thing he'd learned, though, was that Gracie was in no danger. Which was a relief.

ANGUS WATSON STOOD on the front porch of his rented farmhouse, arms akimbo, breathing the fresh country air. The farm itself wasn't as appealing a place to stay as Timberlake Lodge, but the bucolic view of the gently rolling hills surrounding it made up some of the difference.

Angus had spent nearly two of his younger years on a farm. The county juvenile-detention office in the state where he'd been living at the time had been running an experiment. Send troubled youths to a farm, put them to work on the land, doing chores and caring for the animals, and they would learn responsibility and the value of becoming productive members of society. It hadn't worked as far as Angus was concerned. Instead, he'd honed his skills as a budding con artist, learning from the older kids and practicing on the susceptible country kids he went to school with.

He had liked the land, though, and a couple of the animals—Bossy, the old cow he took turns milking, and Andy, an old goat. Bossy liked to wait until an unsuspecting milker was settled, then reach out with her foot and kick away the stool. And Andy loved to sneak up behind people and butt them with his head— hard enough to jolt them off their feet and make their teeth rattle. Both animals seemed to derive some kind of perverse pleasure out of besting people. Maybe that was why Angus had liked them.

Tyler was a long way from northern Louisiana, where Angus had spent his youthful time on the farm, but he supposed farms were similar wherever you were.

A flash of light pierced his eye. Instinctively, he jerked his head.

It was those darned kids again. The ones from the next farm over. For two days now they'd been holed up on top of the highest hill, spying down on him with some kind of telescope. At first he'd wondered if they knew who he was. Then he made himself relax. No one here could know that. He was sure of it. They were just kids, playing.

Still, he found being the object of their attention irritating. Each time he came outside he could feel them watching. It was too close to the way he felt in jail, when his every moment was monitored.

He decided to take the matter into his own hands. He would let them know that he was aware of what they were doing and warn them to knock it off.

Using some of the skills that made him valuable to employers, Angus slipped out of view and was able to make his way around behind the children unobserved.

The two of them were stretched out on the hillside above the farmhouse. Instead of watching him through the telescope that Angus saw was set up on the crest of the hill, they were lying on their backs, legs crossed, staring up at the sky and talking. One, a girl of about ten or eleven, had the brightest, most amazingly colored mop of red hair that Angus had ever seen. It was a riot of pinkish-orange-golden curls cut short around her chubby face. The boy, a couple of years older, was very slim with dark hair.

Before breaking into their idyll, Angus decided to listen. One thing he'd found over the years was that enlightenment sometimes came from the oddest sources and at the oddest times. He'd earned his money more than once by the chance interception of whispered information. And since in her last faxed message Celeste Huntington had doubled her offer if he learned the whereabouts of her grandchild, he was even more anxious to discover what he could.

"He's the sweetest little puppy I've ever seen," the girl was saying. "His ears are so pretty, all curly and soft. I don't see why Mommy wouldn't let me bring him along. I'd watch him. I wouldn't let him run off.''

"Enough talk about your puppy already," the boy groused. "That's all you've been doing since you got him.''

"That's because he's so sweet. I really love him, David. I couldn't have asked for a better birthday present.''

The boy jerked up onto his elbow and leaned threateningly over the girl. "I'm gonna smash you if you keep it up!''

"You wouldn't.''

"I would!''

The girl rolled over onto her stomach and waved her heels back and forth in the air. She didn't seem at all afraid of the threat. "I wonder if he's come back out of his house yet?''

"I doubt it.''

"Well, look.''

"You look.''

"You don't think Matt minds that we're using his telescope, do you?''

"Matt doesn't care about anything right now except playing football.''

"And girls. He cares about girls, especially Tina Mallory.''

"Tina's a cheerleader," David replied, as if that explained everything.

"I think she's also a snob.''

"I didn't say *I* liked her.''

"Who do you like, David? Do you like any girls?''

David crawled forward on his tummy to the telescope. "You think I'd tell you?" he taunted, before adjusting the eyepiece to his eye.

The girl took an impatient breath, but before she could say anything, Angus stepped forward. He'd heard enough to tell him he wasn't going to get any information about Daphne from these two.

"Just *what* do you think you're doing?" he demanded in his best aggrieved tone. "I'm within my rights to call the law, do you know that? This is my property!"

The youngsters scrambled to their feet with huge, startled eyes. They looked at him as if he had two heads. As if, should he make any sudden move, they both would run like deer.

Seconds passed before the boy found his courage. "Naw," he disagreed, "this farm belongs to Judy Lowery."

"I'm renting it, and if I'm renting it, I get to say who comes here."

"Judy lets us play where we want," the girl chimed in, backing up her brother.

Angus stretched to his full five feet, five inches. Frequently his stocky body was mistaken as being soft, but in reality it was mostly hard muscle. "Do I look like a Judy?" he growled. "Now, you two, get lost. And quit spying on me or I'll call your parents. Then if that doesn't do any good, I'll call the cops."

He marched over to the telescope and jerked it off its stand. He then pretended that he was going to throw it.

"No!" they cried in unison, afraid, as he knew they would be, of their older brother's wrath.

He relented. "All right," he said, handing it over. "Just do as I say."

The little girl, her face and body covered with freckles to go along with her amazing hair, looked at him fiercely. "You're not a nice man," she declared. Her blue eyes, the color of a winter sky, were welling with tears.

"No truer words were ever spoken," he said proudly. And he laughed as they walked the first ten feet away from him, then broke into a run.

He doubted that they'd be back.

CHAPTER TEN

GRACIE WALKED ahead of Roger to the table. Somehow it seemed strangely appropriate that they were in the same dining room as the day they'd met. Only instead of being filled with poodle-fanciers, the room was sparsely populated, a reflection of one of the hotel's twice-yearly slow periods, in spring and in fall. It was too early for the snow-lovers and a little too late for summer vacationers.

In one way Gracie was relieved. Fewer people meant fewer wagging tongues. In another way, though, the intimacy of the experience was greatly enhanced. Something she could definitely do without.

Despite Sheila's encouragement, Gracie had almost backed out of coming this evening. She'd picked up the telephone at least three times with the intent of canceling. But what could she say? *I don't want to go out with you because you're far too much of a danger to my peace of mind?*

She hadn't been completely honest with Sheilie, either. She hadn't told her how deeply Roger's kisses disturbed her. Or how much she hadn't wanted them to stop. She had a hard time admitting that to herself!

For everyone's benefit she decided to cling to yesterday's stipulation. They could meet, but only as friends. *Only friends!* she reiterated when, as he took over for the hostess and saw her into her chair, his hand casually brushed her shoulder and caused a tumult of sensation to flood through her body.

His smile was free and easy as he took the chair across from her. He hadn't noticed her reaction. Or had he?

Gracie called herself to task. She had to stop examining every little thing he did! For this evening to work, she had to stop being so aware of him. She had to relax, let go of her worries. Let herself live in the moment and not speculate about the future, or the past. Do as everyone advised and enjoy herself!

"This is very nice," she said, smiling. "I don't like crowds."

"Neither do I," he agreed.

The hostess brought the menus, and Gracie scanned the numerous selections. She wasn't a bit hungry, but she took time mulling over her decision.

The waiter poured their water. The candlelight gave the atmosphere a golden glow. Each table's centerpiece was a bowl of old-fashioned roses, whose sweetness delicately scented the air.

"What looks good to you?" Roger asked.

He'd taken care with his appearance tonight, wearing a dark suit, a white shirt and a burgundy-colored tie. Just as she'd spent time selecting a special dress, one that looked nice on her and was a color that complemented her skin tones—a warm lemon yellow.

"The specialty chicken, I think," she murmured.

"I'm going for the trout."

They gave their orders to the waiter, Gracie deferring to Roger's taste in wine.

It had been a long time since she'd dined this formally. A long time since she'd gone out at all! It felt good to be dressed up and pampered.

"I talked to Britt earlier," he said. "To check how Peter's settling in. She said he'd spent the night in Renee's bed and has hardly been allowed on his feet since. One or the other of them is constantly picking him up."

"Which he probably loves," Gracie said, smiling.

"She said he was starting to bark to be picked up."

"They may have created a monster."

"All the attention will probably be good for him."

The waiter arrived, gained Roger's approval of the wine, then poured each of them a glass. Gracie's fingers wound around the stem, and she tasted it. "Mmm," she murmured. "That's nice, too."

Roger gazed at her over the rim of his glass. Seconds passed before he asked, "So…what have you been doing with yourself today?" But she knew that wasn't his preferred avenue of inquiry. He was merely adhering to her provision, keeping things light.

Gracie shrugged. "Not much. Odds and ends. I went to see Sheila."

"I saw her, too," he said.

Gracie was startled. "You did?"

"Around noon, at the grocery store."

Gracie scaled back her alarm. That was before she and Sheilie had talked. "Oh?"

"She and Douglas were shopping. It's funny. I still

have a hard time not calling him Mr. Wagner. He was my history teacher in high school.''

"He was Sheila's teacher, too."

"I wonder if she got all *A*s."

"Well, she did, but she earned every one. She made *A*s in all her classes."

"I remember. She was two years ahead of me."

"I suppose you did, too?"

Roger leaned back in his chair and smiled. "I had to."

"Because your father wanted you to enter medical school?"

He nodded.

Gracie couldn't help it. She was very aware of how good he looked sitting there. So masculine and in control. His light brown hair was neatly groomed, his sideburns cut perfectly in the latest style. He was freshly shaved, freshly showered. Young. Strong. Virile. What kind of lover would he be? She moved her gaze away.

The soup arrived and Gracie devoted herself to it. Then the waiter appeared with their chicken and trout.

Slowly, ever so slowly as the meal progressed, Gracie began to relax. Roger talked about his experiences in medical school and during his training as a vet, concentrating on the many amusing things that had happened, as well as the odd little idiosyncrasies of some of his teachers. Gracie found herself laughing, once to the point of helpless tears. For her part, she told him some of the funny things that had happened in years past at dog shows she'd attended. How the dogs were the least of the trouble when human egos clashed and trivial fooleries were allowed to grow out of proportion.

It was only when the waiter came to consult them about dessert that Gracie became aware of the passage of time.

She glanced surreptitiously at Roger. He, too, looked relaxed and happy.

"I can't eat another thing," she confessed.

Roger refused dessert as well, and when their bill came, he reached into his jacket for his wallet.

Gracie quickly reached for her purse.

The nearby waiter kept a non-committal face.

"Let me get this, Grace…please," Roger said.

"I only agreed to come if we—"

He slipped a credit card into the leather folder and returned it to the waiter. "We'll settle up another time," he assured her.

"I meant what I said," Gracie insisted.

"I know you did."

Gracie made a mental calculation and extracted a series of bills. She folded them and pushed them across the tablecloth. "I don't like owing people," she said.

He took the bills and tapped them on end before silently slipping them into his pocket.

Gracie should have felt better for her victory, but she didn't. After their nice meal, her stubbornness had returned them to their previous uneasy footing.

Roger signed the credit slip, they collected their coats, then left the hotel—all in a growing silence.

Their footsteps sounded loudly on the parking-lot pavement and reverberated in Gracie's ears. Finally, as they were about to reach the Saturn, she said, "That was a wonderful dinner, Roger. Thank you for—"

Roger urged her toward a path that led away from the parking lot.

"Let's take a walk," he said.

Since Addison Hotels International had taken over the ownership and operation of Timberlake Lodge, extensive work had been done to the surrounding grounds. The rolling hills still retained the feel of a country estate, but a subtle lighting system, hidden among the oaks and maples, provided light on the walking trails at night. Because so few people were staying at the hotel that weekend, Gracie and Roger had the path to themselves.

"Did you hear what I said before?" she asked, hoping for a return to their earlier affability. "I truly did enjoy—"

"When you forgot yourself you did. When you thought about things you didn't."

Gracie chanced a quick look at him. His features were set. "We agreed that I'd pay my part of the dinner," she said. "All I did was—"

He cut her off. "This has nothing to do with money! It's about trust, Gracie."

"Trust?" she echoed.

Roger said nothing for a time. He just continued to walk, Gracie at his side because she couldn't make herself break away.

Finally, as they neared the lake, he turned to face her. "I may be younger than you are, but I'm not stupid. I know when something's happened in a person's life that makes them… You're a lot like Serra, Gracie. You've both gone through a terrible experience, being betrayed by someone you loved. Someone who wasn't worth a second of your time! Maybe that's what she saw in you—a kindred spirit—and that's why she…''

He paused, took a deep breath, then continued in a calmer tone. ''You may not believe this, but I've been in love with you since the first time I saw you. I remember exactly when that was. I'd just started work at the supermarket and I was learning how to pack a bag properly. I wasn't very fast at it and there was a big rush after five. People were short-tempered when they were delayed. And I was delaying them. I could feel Mr. Olsen's eyes boring into the middle of my back. I just knew he was going to let me go. Dad would be humiliated that I hadn't made the grade, and Mom…Mom would be horrified, first that I was there at all—she didn't know about it until later. But her horror would have been even worse if someone inferior—Mr. Olsen was inferior, in her opinion—had fired me.

''Then you walked up to the register. I was bowled over in a second, which made packing your groceries even tougher. I broke two bags trying to do it right. And you…you smiled at me and complimented me for trying so hard. In a voice that Mr. Olsen could hear. He patted me on the back as he went by a little later. I wondered for days if you knew he was watching me and that's why you… Then I decided that you hadn't, that you were just being nice. Afterward, I was your unacknowledged slave.''

Gracie could only stare at him. She searched her memory. She didn't remember the incident. She didn't remember him. The time he was talking about had been a difficult period in her life. She'd moved around on autopilot, just trying to get through the days. But what he'd told her had the ring of truth to it and was so heartbreakingly sweet that she…

He drew her into his arms, as if he'd been doing it all his life. "I've loved you close to forever, Grace. I don't want to be just friends. I want more than that—much more."

Gracie's heart was thudding wildly. She was aware of everything about him—the powerful magnetism of his physical appeal, his unquestioned strength of character, the quiet force of his will, his gentleness.

Sheila had told her not to be afraid of her emotions, not to turn away from them, not to wait until it was too late. Fiona had advised her to ignore convention. What did it matter that twelve years separated them? And that she—the female—was older?

She grew giddy just thinking of the possibilities.

She took the initiative, wrapping her arms around his neck, pressing her body close to his, giving him a series of kisses—short and playful, teasing and tempting. She heard him catch his breath.

Her excitement mounted. Her fingers threaded in his hair. It was soft, like fur. Her body began to tremble.

That was too much for Roger. He took over, murmuring words that were indecipherable, before his lips bore down on hers in a kiss that gave new meaning to the word.

Gracie returned his ardor, touching him, wanting him....

Roger was first to break away. "Grace...we have to stop," he said, his breathing ragged. "Let me take you home...to my home."

Gracie's eyes were soft and unfocused. It felt so wonderful to have his arms wrapped around her, to feel his hot body and coiled muscles. She'd go anywhere with him, feeling like this.

He took her back to his car, which he started and drove away—all the while keeping contact with her by massaging the back of her neck.

Gracie knew she should be thinking sanely. Resurrecting the walls that had kept her safe. But her body had been awakened in a way it hadn't been for years—possibly ever—and she trembled again at the thought of what was yet to come.

It wasn't just sex. Or her need of male companionship. Surprisingly, they had a lot in common. She liked him, liked him a lot, even though she hadn't wanted to and had actively resisted. Could she be falling in love again?

If anything was going to give her pause that night, it was that. Everything was happening so fast! Too fast? Only a short space of time had passed since the dog show, since she'd been steeling herself to meet the people who'd once been a part of the world she and Paul had shared. She'd been unsettled, unnerved, doing the best she could to pretend that her damaged spirit was healed—to little avail, it seemed, from the suppositions and speculations that had gotten back to her. And during that time she'd met Roger. He found her attractive, desirable…but he was young and she was still damaged. Was it right to let things get out of hand too quickly?

Gracie cleared her throat. "Roger…I'm not so sure that this is a good idea. At least, right now."

His hand stopped moving on the back of her neck.

"Everything is happening so fast," she continued. "I—I have to have time to get used to it. I can't… I don't think…"

He frowned. "You're changing your mind?"

"No…yes! I guess. For now. Please try to understand, I…"

He placed both hands on the steering wheel, his grip tight. Suddenly she felt cold.

"I'd like to get my hands on that Paul guy," he said harshly. After a moment he drew a long, steadying breath and said quietly, "All right. We'll wait."

Just as she had once before, Gracie saw Roger in a new light. Upon their first meeting she'd questioned his maturity, and it had nagged at the back of her mind ever since. What he was doing now was about the most mature act she had ever seen. He was putting aside his needs, his desires, for hers. Paul had been five years her senior, yet he had never been so unselfish.

She wanted to slip into Roger's arms again, to let him know how much she appreciated his decision. But if she did that, she didn't trust herself to break away.

Roger drove her home and saw her to her doorstep. "Will you go out with me again, Grace?" he asked, leaning close.

She knew her eyes were filled with warmth. She let him gather her against him. "If you want," she said softly.

"I want," he murmured huskily, and he kissed her, numerous times.

GRACIE'S BODY SANG with the fire of his kisses as she finally let herself into her house and leaned back against the door. A length of time had passed as they stood together on the porch, reluctant to part.

It might have been a dream. What was she, Gracie Lawson, doing feeling this way? Acting this way? At her age she should be able to handle herself with far more decorum. But when he looked at her, when he touched her…

A joy Gracie hadn't felt in years bubbled up in her. She wanted to sing, to dance, to go out into the neighborhood and make everyone as happy as she was. To cry out in sheer exuberance.

Both poodles stood at her feet and looked up at her. Squatting down, she gathered them into her arms, and all the while she hugged them, she laughed.

ROGER TURNED UP the radio in his car. A Motown beat pulsed the windows as he sang along with Stevie Wonder. The music matched his mood perfectly.

Who would have thought, he mused happily as the song came to an end, that by the end of the evening their relationship would have taken such a giant leap forward? That Gracie's "only friends" stance would have crumbled so readily?

They'd come close to destroying it completely. His

body ached when he thought of it. If only they hadn't been out at the lake. If only he hadn't pulled back, wanting their first lovemaking to be a little more private…

She'd wanted it, too. She'd openly wanted him.

He let out a whoop in celebration, then laughed when he saw that the driver in the next car was looking at him.

Roger smiled hugely and waved.

So what if one of his clients thought he'd gone temporarily insane!

ROGER'S GOOD MOOD lasted all the way home. He parked the Saturn in the garage next to the van, made his way to his house, whistling the earlier Stevie Wonder tune, and then heard it—the ringing telephone.

Damn! he muttered under his breath. He'd traded off with the vet in Sugar Creek that night. He wasn't supposed to get any emergency calls.

The telephone didn't stop ringing.

Roger fumbled with the key, then pushed his way inside. On the way to the wall phone, he stubbed his toe on the corner of a counter.

"Hello!" he barked shortly, his foot smarting. "Animal Crackers."

"Roger?" a mature, feminine voice said. A voice he had known all his life.

"Mother?" he queried. His mind raced to make adjustments. It wasn't a call about an injured pet or a pet that had fallen ill. He juggled the phone as he shucked off his coat, tossing it over the back of the nearest chair. "Is that you?"

"Well, of course it is," she responded primly. "Who did you think it was? You have only one mother."

"Yes, but…" He stopped himself. Most times, he had learned over the years, it paid not to get into an argument with his mother. She had a set way of thinking, and Mount Vesuvius exploding right in her face could barely gain her attention if she was determined not to notice. He pulled a second chair closer and sat down. This could take a while. "How are you?" he asked. "It's been a long time."

"Yes, it has. It wouldn't hurt you to call more often. I might have died, and would you care?"

"Of course I'd care."

"You don't act like it.

"I'll try to do better," he promised, knowing that he should.

"All right, then," she agreed.

A silence settled over the line. Roger waited for his mother to collect her thoughts, but when the moments ticked by and she said nothing else, he asked carefully, "Mom…is there something wrong?"

"I'd like you to come to Chicago, Roger. I want to see you."

"I'd like to come, too, Mom," he hedged, "but things are really busy around here. I can't get away right now. I—"

"I want you to come as soon as you can, Roger. It's important."

"What's this about, Mom?" he asked, afraid that

he already knew. The trouble his father was causing Melissa. Or at least, the trouble she *thought* he was causing. Roger had already talked to his dad, and George denied calling Missy's husband to enlist his help with the boys. "Is it about Missy and—"

"Hush! I don't want you to say that man's name in my presence! Not after the trouble he's caused! First he abandons me for that hussy Marge Peterson, then he tries to break up Missy's marriage." She drew a deep breath, obviously trying to calm herself. "I didn't mean to get into that. It's not your fault, neither is it Missy's. We all know where the blame lies. I called because I'm trying to repair the damage he's doing. Missy is miserable, Roger. I'm afraid this could destroy her relationship with John. He's on his high horse, she's on hers. I can't stand to see the children torn apart. You just don't know how many times I thank God that you and Missy were grown up and out of the house before your father decided to…" She took another calming breath. "So I decided to see if there was anything I could do. That's why I want to talk to you. I have an idea."

"An idea?" Roger repeated. Sometimes his mother's ideas were a little strange.

"Come see me tomorrow, or Tuesday, and I'll tell you about it. But don't leave it too late. I'm feeling the tiniest bit charitable now. It may not last."

Roger leaned forward in the chair. That his mother had made the offer was amazing. Off the wall or not, her idea deserved to be heard. And he knew from past experience that if she wanted to speak to him in person, he would have to present himself. Who knew?

Maybe this idea would be good for her as well as the rest of them. Because, no matter what she said to the contrary, *she* was the one responsible for most of the trouble that had occurred since she and their father had separated.

"I'll be there as soon as I can," he promised. "Not tomorrow. I know I can't get anyone to cover the clinic. But I'll try for Tuesday."

"Do that," his mother instructed. And before she hung up, she said with less certainty, "You do still love me, don't you, Roger?"

"Of course I love you," Roger was quick to answer. Only to himself did he add guiltily, *but you'd be a lot easier to love if you weren't so demanding.*

Serra had heard him come in and had padded downstairs to greet him. Now, when he finally noticed her after hanging up the phone, she rested her chin on his thigh as she leaned against him, her beautiful brown eyes rolling back to look at him.

He rubbed her ear. "You know better than most about the ups and downs of life, don't you, girl? One minute you're in the clouds because something unbelievably wonderful has happened. The next, you come crashing back to earth, flat on your back."

Serra gave a soft whimper of understanding.

Roger stroked her silky hair. "I guess all we can do is try to roll with it," he mused. "And hope that the good isn't some kind of illusion.

"Come on," he said, standing up, "let's get you outside for a walk."

Serra gave a happy bark and wagged her tail in agreement.

CHAPTER ELEVEN

GRACIE AWOKE the next morning in just as happy a mood as when she had gone to sleep the previous night. Even her dreams had been pleasant. She felt vibrant and energetic, ready to face the future. No longer was she afraid to look forward. Good things were out there waiting for her. Wonderful things!

Gracie gave a delighted laugh, feeling more like her old self than she had in ages. She wondered when she would hear from Roger, then castigated herself for wondering. He had said he would call when he had a chance, and he would.

In the meantime she busied herself with her scheduled duties. She checked the well-being of her elders, delivered meals to shut-ins and was on her way to the library to read to the children when the telephone rang.

Her hand trembled lightly as she answered it, then trembled even more when she heard Roger's voice.

"I wish I could come over right now and see you," he said softly, intimately.

She groped for a chair and clumsily settled into it. "I wish you could, too. I...you just caught me. I was on my way out the door. I'm going to the library to read to five-year-olds."

"What will you read to them? Cinderella? Sleeping Beauty? Snow White?"

She smiled. "Actually, the last time we were together, I promised to read about a helicopter named Budgie."

"Don't kids like fairy tales anymore?"

"Did you?"

"I still like them," he said, and the warm promise in his voice made Gracie's toes curl. "Do you have to leave right away?" he asked.

Reluctantly, she checked her watch. "I should already be gone."

He sighed. "Me, too. I just finished some minor surgery on a Persian and need to go check on her. But this is the only time I'm going to get to talk to you for a day or two. Something's come up and I have to go to Chicago."

Gracie felt a stab of disappointment. "Oh?"

"To visit my mom. She called and wants to see me."

She could sense a certain tenseness in his tone. "Is something wrong?" she asked. "Is she ill?"

"No. It's just…family stuff. You know."

Gracie felt a little put off. He didn't want to tell her.

He interpreted her short silence correctly because he added, "It has to do with a problem between my dad and my sister. Everyone seems to think I can fix it. I'll drive down tonight and come back for Wednesday."

"What about the clinic?"

"Fiona's rescheduling tomorrow's appointments,

and I'll get Matt Johnston in Sugar Creek to fill in on emergencies. He owes me a couple.''

Everything was being taken care of. So why did Gracie feel this growing emptiness? Because he was going away?

She forced herself to say something. ''Well, be careful.''

''I will. I'll call you on Wednesday.''

Gracie nodded, and he seemed somehow to know.

''I'll see you then,'' he said.

He might have stayed talking longer, except Gracie heard Fiona's voice in the background, calling to him. He hung up the phone.

Slowly, she hung up as well. A bit of the bloom had faded from her rose. The day suddenly didn't seem as bright.

GRACIE STAYED BUSY the rest of the day. She tried not to let herself have time to think about Roger and how rapidly he had come to mean something to her. She volunteered for extra duty at the animal shelter and spent most of the afternoon and early evening there.

When she arrived home, her own dogs wanted attention. She took them for a long walk, then brushed their coats.

She was just putting the brush away when the phone rang.

''Gracie!'' Fiona cried. ''I'm so glad I finally reached you!''

It was silly, but for a moment Gracie's heart was gripped by fear. ''What's wrong?'' she asked quickly.

"You know that Dr. Phelps has gone to Chicago."

"I know."

"And being that that's true, I'd like to talk to you about it sometime. I saw the way he looked when he was talking to you. Kinda loopy, like a lovesick—"

"Fiona!"

Her old friend chuckled. "You're right. I'm wasting my time. He won't tell me what's going on, either. I'm just happy to see that *something* is!" She paused for breath. "Anyway, I was wondering if I could ask a favor. Since the clinic is closed tomorrow and I have an unexpected day off, I was wondering if I could ask you to watch out for Serra in the afternoon and evening. I told Dr. Phelps I wouldn't have any problem doing it, but I talked to my sister in Milwaukee, and she has some tickets to a musical that we've both been dying to see and—"

"You don't have to say another word," Gracie interrupted. "I'd be happy to take care of Serra. If you think it wouldn't upset her."

"That's wonderful! Thanks! I won't be leaving until after lunch. If you could stop by the clinic while I'm there, I'll show you the routine. And as far as Serra goes…remember, she's already shown she likes you. That's the main reason I thought of you. You don't have to stay with her, of course. Just drop by a couple of times to feed her and let her out."

"Not a problem," Gracie assured her.

Gracie went about the evening's chores—straightening the house, cooking up a few things that she would eat over the next few days. Maybe she would ask Roger over one evening after he returned and cook a meal for him. A whisper of anticipation at seeing him again slid along her spine.

After she went to bed she speculated, as she had earlier, about where he might be at this moment. Had he already arrived safely in Chicago? The sprawling metropolis to the south was no more than an hour and a half away from Tyler by car.

She also thought about Mary Phelps, Roger's mother. Gracie had a spotty memory of the woman. The last time she recalled seeing her, Mary had had light brown hair, was perfectly groomed, displayed good taste in clothes and sported what for Tyler was a haughty expression. She seemed to revel in her position in the community, earned by her marriage into the Phelps family.

The Phelpses had been important in Tyler for many years, what with Roger's great-uncle Zachary's years of service as police chief and later his representation on the town council. Zachary's older sister Tillie had been a leader, as well, until she'd been forced to retire. Then there was George, Mary's husband and Roger's father, and his position at the hospital.

Through marriage, Mary had possessed all the necessary social credentials, which she'd played to the hilt. Grande dame that she was, though, Mary wasn't very well-liked. She had a hard time relating to people on a one-to-one basis.

At a certain point Gracie had lost track of her, not being particularly interested in her exploits. Now she wished she had paid greater attention. Bits and pieces of gossip had filtered out of Tyler during the breakup of the marriage and Mary's eventual bitter departure, but Gracie could only remember a few.

Gracie thumped her pillow and adjusted it behind her head. She'd had no idea that George Phelps and his daughter were having trouble, but it didn't surprise her. She knew Melissa had sided with her mother. How did Roger feel about the breakup? He was friends with Raine Peterson, Marge's daughter. Did that mean he disapproved less? Or that he had learned to live with it? Maybe that was why he saw himself as being older emotionally, because he'd had to live through so much strife.

Roger…if he was here with her right now she would hold him close and offer comfort.

Roger…here with her.

Gracie groaned and once again adjusted the pillow.

THE NEXT MORNING, as Gracie parked her car outside the church activity building where the meals for shut-ins were prepared, she noticed a couple of people eyeing her. When she smiled, they quickly turned away. It happened several more times, at various places, throughout the morning. It took that long for Gracie to realize what the sudden interest was about—word must be spreading around Tyler about her and Roger having dinner together.

It was nearly one o'clock when Gracie parked the Miata outside the veterinary clinic and hurried onto the porch. The door was locked when she tried it. She rang the bell, then stepped out into the yard when Fiona popped open a window on the second floor.

"Come around back," she called, while pointing toward a gate in the fence.

Gracie followed the flagstone path to the gate and let herself through. In a way it felt as if she was intruding into Roger's life. But he had wanted to bring her here Sunday night, had been disappointed when she'd refused.

Fiona met her at the back door with a cheery smile. "Hello!" she called. "I'd just about given up on you!"

"I'm running late, as usual," Gracie murmured, glancing around the nicely appointed backyard. Mature trees shaded a large portion of the area, from the side of the garage to the house and out to where a run had been built between the house and the far fence. Near the back door, white chairs and a table sat on a low wooden deck.

"Can't be helped sometimes," Fiona said, opening the door wider for her to come inside. "I'm not in a particular rush. Just so long as I get there by four. Jill wants to have dinner before the show."

"Which show is it?" Gracie asked.

"A touring company of *Phantom of the Opera*. I've wanted to see it for ages, but I never thought I'd get the chance."

"Lucky you!" Gracie said.

Fiona gave her a close look. "I've been hearing a few very interesting things on the gossip line."

"I'm sure you have."

She led the way upstairs. "Doesn't it bother you?"

"All we did was have dinner."

"That's not what I heard," Fiona teased.

Gracie thought of the time by the lake and the time they'd spent on her front porch. Someone must have seen them.

The entire downstairs portion of the house was devoted to the clinic. Roger's private domain was on the upper floor. Once again, Gracie felt as if she were an invader. From the way newspapers and opened mail were scattered on the kitchen table and a small collection of dishes were rinsed but not washed in the sink, he hadn't expected company. All in all, though, he was very neat. The wood floors were shiny, the rugs vacuumed, the shelves free of dust.

Gracie continued to look around. The place had a definite masculine atmosphere, but one in which a woman could feel at ease. He liked warm, rich, earth-tones and muted whites. Photographs and plaques covered one wall, but from a distance Gracie couldn't identify them.

Serra, on second look, was hiding under the table. "Her usual place when I come upstairs," Fiona said. "I don't understand it. I *love* animals. I wouldn't hurt one if someone paid me! But she won't let me touch her for anything. I've tried and tried. And to make matters worse, she scoots under the table and won't come out unless I walk away. She makes me feel like an ax-murderer or something."

"I'm sure it's not personal," Gracie murmured, bending down to call a soft hello to the dog, who returned her look levelly. "Maybe she just needs more time."

"I'm not sure it'll ever get any better!" Fiona complained. "Right now, though, I can't worry about it.

Here, let me show you...." She went on to explain Serra's schedule and show Gracie where everything of importance to the dog was kept.

"She'll need to be fed at six and taken outside for a play in the yard. I've already taken her for her noon outing. Then—and I know this is hard—she needs to be let out one more time around ten. Otherwise, she has a hard time making it through the night. Usually, if she doesn't get it, she'll have an accident and be so upset that...it's just far easier to take her out at ten."

"I don't mind," Gracie said.

Fiona frowned, trying to think if she'd forgotten anything. "Dr. Phelps said he'd probably be back sometime late tonight—around one or two was his estimate. He always has a hard time breaking away from his mother. The woman just can't seem to understand that he has other obligations. I'll be back around that time myself, so I'll call first thing in the morning and be sure he got home. Otherwise, I'll come over and see to Serra myself. You won't need to worry." She looked gratefully at Gracie. "I can't tell you what this means to me. It's so—"

Gracie herded her toward the stairs. "You'd better get going. Otherwise you'll be late, too."

Fiona dangled a key ring. "Keys to the house," she managed to say before reaching the stairs.

"I'll take wonderful care of Serra," Gracie said, accepting them. "You enjoy yourself!"

"I will. Oh, I will!"

Gracie had just turned away when Fiona called up

to her. "Dr. Johnston from Sugar Creek is standing in...in case you need him. His number—"

"Fiona, I know his number. He's the boys' vet."

Fiona blinked at her, then started to laugh. Gracie could hear her chuckling all the way to the door.

Gracie was very aware of Serra's eyes fastened on her as she came back to the table and bent down. As she had once before, she extended a curled hand for the dog to sniff.

"We're going to do just fine, aren't we, girl?" she said softly. "I'm going away right now, but I'll be back later."

When Gracie withdrew her hand, Serra belly-crawled a few inches forward, allowing herself to be more visible.

"I'll be back," Gracie repeated.

Serra dropped her head to the floor and waited for Gracie to leave. She'd made the only concession she planned to at the moment.

"Mom," Roger said with strained patience, "I didn't come all this way to listen to you tear down Dad. You said you had an idea."

"I do," Mary Phelps said.

His mother's posture was regal as usual as she sat in one of the Chippendale chairs Roger remembered from childhood. At the time of the divorce she had insisted upon taking all the furniture. Visiting her in her apartment was like stepping back in time to their old home.

"I merely want you to understand what a great sacrifice I'm prepared to make," his mother said. "Your father doesn't deserve it, but in order to preserve Melissa's marriage…''

Roger gritted his teeth.

''I'm willing to intervene.''

Roger waited for more. When it didn't come, he asked carefully, ''Intervene in what way?''

''Melissa will do as I say. If I tell her to allow her father to visit the boys, she will.''

Roger blinked. Is this what his mother wouldn't tell him on the phone? What she had dragged him all the way to Chicago to say? Anger bubbled up inside him, anger that he tried to suppress.

''Mom,'' he began tightly, ''you could have done that months ago and saved us all a lot of trouble.''

''I'm not doing it to save your father trouble.''

''Mom!'' Some of his frustration slipped through. ''I didn't say only Dad. I said *us all!* Melissa, John, the children, me. You, even!''

''Me?'' his mother repeated. ''I don't know what you're talking about, Roger. If you're going to say something, you simply must make yourself clear. It isn't proper to leave people to guessing. It's rude. It's—''

Roger's temper snapped. He jerked to his feet and stood over her, his hands curling tightly. If she hadn't been his mother, he might have shaken her.

''Then let me be very clear, shall I?'' he said. ''But you're going to have to open your ears. I want you to hear every word, because, Mom, this is the only time I'm ever going to say it.'' He took a quick breath. ''You need to stop making your world revolve around Dad. For your sake—for everyone's sake!—

you have to make the final break and let go! I don't
know what went wrong in your marriage. You and
Dad…were you ever truly happy with each other? I
don't want an answer, I just want you to think about
it. If the answer's no, then you've already spent far
too many years in the pursuit of nothing. And you
can't get those years back! No matter how hard you
try, no matter how many people you hurt in the pro-
cess.''

His mother's mouth twitched, her expression
daunting. Still, she remained silent.

Some of his anger dissipated and Roger dropped
down on his knees beside his mother's chair. He
reached out to take her hands in his. Her fingers were
icy. ''Mom,'' he pleaded softly. ''For your sake…so
you can find happiness somewhere before it's too
late…let go of the past. Let go of Dad.''

A muscle jumped in his mother's arm, and her lips
twitched again. ''You always did take his side,'' she
said in a choked voice.

Roger massaged her fingers, trying to bring warmth
to them. He hated to be so blunt, but he could see
that his mother's offer to make peace was only another attempt at manipulation. It was a game she was
playing, where she could use the power she had over
Missy to control her ex-husband. She could give access to his grandchildren and she could take it away,
whenever the whim struck.

''I'm not taking sides, Mom,'' he insisted. ''I'm
just trying to make you see clearly, like you said. I
want you to be happy.''

''I wish I could believe that, Roger.''

"I can't make you believe me. That's something only you can do yourself."

"You hate my idea," she said tonelessly.

"Only because it continues the cycle. It's a way of striking back at Dad. As long as you control Missy, you control him. The best thing you can do, Mom, is encourage Missy to think for herself. She's an adult! She's twenty-nine! Don't you think it's time to cut the apron strings? She's not a child anymore. She has children of her own. A husband…and a life."

"Now you want me to reject my daughter," his mother accused, tears forming in her eyes.

"No, I didn't say that." Roger felt like he was making a hash of everything. The way things were turning out, he should have made some excuse and stayed at home. He should have let the situation play itself out. Like a fire raging in an open oil tank, it would eventually burn itself out if left alone. Possibly to the detriment of everything around it, but sometimes a person had no other choice. Rushing in to battle it alone, a person took the chance of being consumed.

"That's what it sounded like to me, Roger!" his mother said.

Roger tried again. He had to give it one final try. "Mom, think about it," he urged. "You have a good brain, you have talent. You can organize social affairs better than anyone I've ever seen. Take that ability and *do* something with it! I'll bet you could flip some of these Chicago society ladies on their ears in ten seconds flat."

Much to his surprise, a smile trembled on his

mother's lips. She liked the verbal picture he had drawn, and she liked the compliment.

"You can do it, Mom!" he continued. "Whatever you set your mind to, you can do!" Then he took a chance. "And you don't need Dad to make it happen. Think about this for a second: Dad is like a weight you carry around with you all the time. Get rid of him, push him away...and see how much easier life is for you. You'll be able to walk! To run! To dance and play! Wouldn't you like to be able to play, Mom?"

For a second he was afraid that he had overdone it. The obstinate look had settled back on her face. Her jaw had tightened, lifted. Then, like an old, over-stretched rubber band breaking, the tension snapped and released.

"You make it sound so easy," she whispered huskily.

"I wish it was. It would be wonderful if problems could be solved so easily. Not doing this—not hitting out like you planned—is only the first step, Mom. You're going to need some outside help. You're going to need someone to talk to, someone to help you find the way."

"A psychiatrist. Is that what you're saying? You think I'm crazy!"

He smiled and squeezed her hands. "I think I'd call it *determined.* And no, not anything as formal as a psychiatrist. A counselor is what most people call them. Someone to help you work things out."

His mother looked at him for a long time, and Roger waited.

Eventually she asked, "Where did I get such a brilliant son?"

He flashed a grin. "I'm a doctor, remember?"

"Yes, for cats and dogs."

"We all have feelings, Mom."

"I've always wanted the best for you. For both you and Melissa," she said quietly.

Roger stood up. "What say we go talk to her?"

His mother looked up at him blankly. "I thought you didn't want me to."

"I didn't mean ever again," Roger teased. "I meant, not in the way you intended. Then, after that, what's the name of the best restaurant in town? I'm in the mood to host a really nice meal for the ladies of my family. Then maybe we can play tourist and go sightseeing. That is, if both of you would like to come out with me."

His mother's smile grew stronger. "I'm sure we would." Then, showing that she'd taken Roger's advice to heart, she amended, "But then, I can't speak for Melissa."

Roger leaned over and gave her cheek a light kiss. He had no idea how long her agreeableness would last, but at least they had made some progress.

GRACIE WATCHED Serra walk back upstairs from her ten o'clock outing, the limp making her list a little to one side. Moments before, Gracie had been allowed to pet her, and as she stroked the silky hair, she'd felt the scars beneath the beautiful golden coat.

How could anyone treat an animal badly? Gracie wondered. What kind of subhuman would do that?

As far as she was concerned, people who mistreated an animal should receive the same punishment as they would if they'd mistreated a fellow human. In some cases, their punishment should be even harsher, because animals place their full trust in people and rely on them for care. Gracie thought of the drifter who had abused Serra so heartlessly and wished that she could do a little abusing herself.

Serra, already at the upper landing, turned to look at her, almost as if she'd sensed her thoughts. It was a spooky feeling to have a dog gaze at you and convey the idea that she had long ago forgiven the person who'd abused her, because that was an essential part of a dog's makeup—to forgive.

Gracie had to clear the lump of emotion from her throat before she could speak as she joined Serra on the landing. "How about another dog biscuit, girl? I think you deserve one."

Serra's ears lifted and she stood a little taller. Gracie went into the kitchen, to the cabinet where the doggie treats were stored.

Serra took the biscuit from her fingers with ladylike reticence, then plopped down on the nearest rug to eat it.

As Gracie closed the cabinet, she caught sight again of the photographs and plaques that decorated one wall. Nonchalantly, she went to examine them. Some were family photos, showing George and Mary and their two children in a studio pose. Roger was about ten years old in one and a little older in another. He was handsome even then. Another photo showed him in a high-school track uniform, ready to vault over a high bar, his pole bent as he ascended feet first into the air. Another was of a group of skiing buddies—he was in the middle—their faces bright with laughter.

There were pictures of other people, as well, caught as they went about their everyday life in what looked like villages in Europe. In the background were houses with flowers blooming in window boxes, a stone fountain flowing with water in a plaza. The plaques, she now saw, honored both serious and gag accomplishments.

People and places and things from Roger's life, a life she had no part of. Just as he had no part of large sections of her own life. Particularly her time with Paul.

Gracie pushed Paul out of her mind and curled into the comfortably stuffed chair closest to where Serra lay stretched out on the rug.

She would stay for a little while, to keep Serra company. The dog missed Roger when he was away…just as she was coming to realize that she did, too.

CHAPTER TWELVE

GRACIE CAME AWAKE to the sound of footsteps approaching from a distance. She sat up, confused. She wasn't in her bed. She wasn't in her house. She was in a chair—a chair that wasn't her own! Memory was just returning when the overhead light came on.

"Ahh!" she cried reflexively, cringing.

"What the—" Roger exclaimed, startled.

"Wuf," Serra contributed, her head high.

Then Roger started to laugh. He laughed so hard that he sank down onto the landing, one leg extended along the stairs, the other foot propped on a step for added purchase.

"My God," he said at last, "that took a few years off my expected life span!"

Gracie peered across the room. "Roger? That is you, isn't it?"

He pushed to his feet and came over to her, taking time to pat Serra's head. "Of course it's me. Did you think I was the bogeyman?"

Gracie smiled as she struggled to sit up. "What time is it?" she asked, still a little fuzzy.

"A few minutes after eleven."

"You're back early. At least, from what Fiona said—"

He eased himself onto the arm of the chair and leaned over to kiss the top of her head. "Were you waiting for me?" he asked, sounding pleased.

His nearness made her heart beat faster. "No, actually, I was sitting with Serra. I was going to keep her company for a little while, then...I must have fallen asleep."

"Not that I'm complaining, but what are you doing here?"

"Fiona asked if I'd sub for her this evening. Her sister had tickets for a musical and invited her to come along."

"I didn't see your car."

Gracie shrugged. "It's out there...in front, along the street."

"I guess I missed it because I wasn't looking."

He stood up, pulled her up, too, then took her place in the chair, bringing her back with him, to sit on his lap. It happened so quickly Gracie couldn't protest.

"I like it that you were waiting for me," he murmured. "I could get used to it very fast." He paused, then said in an even softer voice, "I missed you."

"You were only gone for a day," Gracie teased.

"Did you miss me?"

"One day, Roger. That's not exactly—"

"*Did* you miss me?" He wasn't going to let her evade answering.

"Would it make you happy if I said yes?"

"Only if you meant it."

She tried to wiggle free. "Roger, I have to go. You might not have seen my car, but other people will."

"So what?"

"So…we're already the prime subject of conversation in town. Did you know that? Do you want it to get worse?"

"I don't care." His brown eyes were warm with lazy appreciation as his fingers played in the feathery ends of her hair. "Would it solve the difficulty if I asked you to marry me?"

Gracie blinked. "I—I'd say you were rushing things."

"Fourteen years is a long time to think about something."

"Roger—"

"I know this isn't what you asked, but…" He cupped his hand at the back of her neck and brought her face down to his. Their lips met lightly at first, then with growing ardor.

Gracie couldn't stop herself. The intimacy of their position was breathtaking—her body curled against his in the cocoon of the overstuffed chair, making her wholly aware of his need of her. Aware that, as she arched back, inviting him to bury his face in the hollow between her breasts, they were dangerously close to losing all reason.

Yet when he stood up, lifting her with him, to take the few steps into his bedroom, Gracie managed to break it off.

"Roger…stop!" she panted. "We can't…"

"I want to marry you, Grace."

"No…no! It's not as simple as that! I wish it were. But nothing's changed, Roger. Nothing—"

"I love you. And I think, if you'd let yourself, you'd love me, too."

Gracie struggled to keep her thoughts on track. She spoke aloud some of her previous reasoning. "We—we have to look at the situation clearly! You're young. What you feel for me might be a passing fancy. A dalliance with an older woman. You said it yourself—you had a crush! Maybe—maybe that's all this is now, too, only you don't know it. And in a few months—a few weeks even!—you could feel differently."

"Clearly." Roger put her down as he zeroed in on the word. "Why do women want everything to be *clear,* then won't listen?"

Gracie didn't understand the question, or how it applied to her. "Roger, I—"

"My mother wanted me to speak clearly, too. But she didn't like what she heard when I did. It went against her preconceived notion of how her life was ordered." He looked at Gracie through narrowed eyes, his body taut. "You want to know why I don't care about what other people say? It's because that's all my mother ever cared about. Convention was her god—what people thought, what people said. She wouldn't make a move if she thought it would tarnish her image in the community. And, not content to worry about it only for herself, she worried about it for Missy and me, too. I caught hell when I worked that summer at Olsen's Supermarket. It wasn't proper for the son of people of such high rank to be rubbing elbows with the lower classes. She sacrificed everything she ever had on the altar of convention—even her marriage."

Gracie looked at him. This was the first real insight she'd had into his relationship with his family.

"There is a middle ground," was all that she could say in defense of her prior worry.

"Not for me," he said. "I made up my mind a long time ago that other people's pettiness wasn't going to affect the way I live my life. Particularly not in the things I think are important."

"I'm not accustomed to being talked about, Roger. My family—" She had been going to say, *was too emotionally stilted to ever draw attention to themselves,* but he interrupted her.

"What do you feel for me, Grace—nothing?"

Gracie was appalled. She couldn't believe that he would think she could be so intimate with someone she didn't even like. "Roger, that's not... Of course I like you!"

"Only *like?*"

Gracie turned away. How could she assure him of anything else? Once, she'd thought she was in love with Paul. It had seemed real at the time. Now Paul had been relegated to a memory—and a bad one at that!

"You have to understand," she pleaded, turning back to him. "This is a strange time in my life. I'm up in the air about everything! I just gave up a business that was my dream, and I haven't found anything to put in its place! I like you, Roger. I like you a lot. I might even... But I don't know for sure yet. And I can't take that kind of chance. It hurts when you make a wrong decision. It hurts for a long time. Please? Try to understand?"

A humorless smile touched his lips. "Our relationship is really one for the books, isn't it? I, the male, am considered immature because I'm younger. You, the older female, are considered totally responsible. Yet I'm the one who wants to commit, and you're the one who wants to preserve your options. Maybe we should call one of the television talk shows and volunteer to be guests."

"Don't insult me, Roger. It's more than that."

"And you haven't insulted me?" Again he focused on one word. "You as good as told me I can't separate my sexual urges from my true feelings. And that if we slept together a few times, I'd be sated and ready to move on!"

"That's *not* what I—"

"It sure as hell *is* what you said."

"Well, I didn't mean it that way!" Gracie stamped a foot in frustration. "Oh, this is hopeless! We haven't even gotten together yet…and still we—"

"I know one way to prove you wrong," he interrupted. "Sleep with me. And since you're so sensitive to what other people say, we can arrange it so no one knows. We can go to Madison or Milwaukee or even Chicago. We'll stay for a week, and at the end of that time, we'll talk."

The idea was so audacious that Gracie could only stare at him.

"What's the matter?" he taunted, smiling. "Cat got your tongue?"

GRACIE DROVE HOME in a state of emotional turmoil, and she stayed that way throughout the night and into the next day. She hadn't hung around long after Roger issued his challenge. She was afraid he might try to bundle her off against her will and put his words to the test.

He swore he loved her. But did he? He'd asked her to marry him. But did he mean it? And did she mean what she'd said?

What she'd told him was the truth. Her entire life felt as if it was spinning out of orbit. It had been barely two months since she'd left the kennel for the last time and moved into town. She'd only just finished decorating the house she planned to live in for a year. After that, she still didn't know.

One thing she did know, though. She'd never included getting involved with a younger man in her plans—or any man, for that matter. She needed time to think, to assess. And she couldn't do that lying in his bed, being held in his arms!

"Do you still see him?" Renee asked, scratching the itch that lying on her tummy in the grass and dirt had caused. "Is he still on the porch?"

"Yep," David answered, keeping his eyes plastered to the binoculars they had borrowed from their father. "That lady just left again…the one with the realty-company sign on her car. I wonder why she comes so much?"

"Maybe she wants to marry him," Renee speculated.

"She'd have to be crazy!" David said scornfully.

"She doesn't know who he is, does she? She probably thinks he's really nice."

"I still say she'd have to be crazy!" David sniffed.

They had changed their base of operation since their run-in with their neighbor. This view wasn't as good as the one before, but it was shielded by a large clump of bushes.

The cocker puppy, frolicking after a windblown leaf, pulled on his leash. *"Errr-ruf!"* he half growled, half barked.

"Keep him quiet!" David ordered.

"He's getting bored…just like I am," Renee complained.

"Being a spy isn't easy work."

"I'm not a spy, and neither are you."

David dropped his forehead to his arm. "If you don't stop saying that…!"

"Well, we aren't!"

"We're watching him for Mom and for Brick."

"Watching him do what? Sit a while and then leave? That's all he ever does."

David went back to the binoculars. "It's still important."

"I think we should go talk to him."

"No," David answered with barely contained patience. "Mom said we had to stay away from him. Anyway, I don't remember you wanting to hang around and talk when he surprised us the other day."

"I didn't say I *wanted* to talk to him," Renee answered with a touch of disdain. "I said I thought maybe we should."

"What good would that do?"

"We might get him to tell us something by accident."

"*What* would he tell us?"

"I don't know. Something."

"Then see what a stupid idea it is! You wouldn't know if he told you anything important, even if he did. All that would happen is we'd get into trouble…just like we would have done if we'd told Mom about him catching us out. She wouldn't let us come again. She…" David stopped talking as something bright and close by blurred his view through the binoculars. "Get down!" he ordered, and took his own advice. Then he saw that his sister was no longer there, and that it had been her bright red skirt swishing in the breeze that had blotted out his field of vision. Carrying the little dog, she was heading down the hill toward the farmhouse. "Renee!" he called with as much force as he could muster while trying to keep his voice from carrying. "Get back here! Get back here right now! Don't be really stupid and—"

She turned around and stuck her tongue out at him, then continued on her way.

David gritted his teeth and hurried to intercept her. "Renee. Renee! I'll tell Mom. She'll get really mad and…and maybe take your puppy away!"

"Mommy wouldn't do that," she retorted.

She stomped on and David followed her, not wanting to, yet at the same time unwilling to let her go on alone.

Renee didn't stop until she stood at the porch. The man was sitting in a chair, sleeping. At least, he seemed to be sleeping—until one eye popped open, then the next.

He sat up with a jerk. "What the—?"

"Hello," Renee said pleasantly.

Angus Watson looked from the girl to the boy and back again, then he shook his head briskly.

"We thought we'd come to say hello," she continued.

Angus frowned. "All right, you have," he growled. "Now go away."

Renee cocked her head. "Why are you so grumpy?" she asked.

"Because some little kids from next door keep giving me trouble."

"We're your neighbors. You're supposed to be friends with your neighbors."

"I don't want any friends." He stood up, and the boy edged closer to his sister, as if to protect her.

"This is my new puppy," Renee said, looking down at the spaniel. "His name's Peter." She offered the dog for his approval.

Angus recoiled. "Get that thing away from me!" he yelled.

Renee pulled the puppy close and looked hurt.

"You're not afraid of a puppy, are you?" David spoke for the first time. He put all the scorn of a twelve-year-old into the question.

Angus glared at him. "I'm not afraid of nothing, kid."

"Then why—"

Angus's loud sneeze rent the air. "That's why, kid. Now, get it away from me!"

David grinned. "You're allergic! Yeah!"

Angus dragged a hankie from his back pocket and blew his nose. He mumbled something unintelligible.

David motioned for Renee to back up. She sent him a hard look, but did as he directed.

"Okay," he said. "She's back now."

Angus gave them both a sour look. "I meant all the way back...to your farm, both of you."

"What kind of a name is Angus?" David asked curiously, starting to enjoy the tête-à-tête his sister had arranged.

Angus looked surprised. "You know my name?"

"Word gets around out here."

Angus's eyes narrowed. "What else do you know?"

"Only that you're some kind of rich big shot on a long vacation," David replied.

"*And* that you're allergic to dogs," Renee added. "And that you don't like people."

"Angus. Is that your real name?" David asked again.

"As real as they come, kid."

"Do you have a nickname?"

Angus hitched up his pants and threw them an irritated look. "I don't have time for this!" he grumbled.

"My nickname's Button," Renee confided. "And his—" she indicated her brother "—his is Skip. We don't use them all the time, just sometimes...when we feel like it."

"Is your nickname even worse than your real name?" David probed. "Is that why you won't—"

"In some circles I'm known as The Stump, okay? But I only let my best friends call me that!"

"Why The Stump?" Renee asked, frowning.

"Because The Flower just wouldn't work!" Angus exclaimed mockingly. "Now you two get going. I'm busy."

"You don't look busy," Renee said.

Angus's mouth tightened. "How many times do I have to say it?"

"You could be a nice man if you wanted to," Renee replied quietly. "Mommy says it's far easier to be nice than it is to be mean. *And* you can sleep at night. Do you sleep good at night, Mr. Stump?"

Angus had had enough. More than enough. He started to growl deep in his throat, then he lunged at them, coming off the porch in an angry rush.

His sudden threat startled the children, making the girl scream and the boy yip. They wheeled and ran, but a few steps later the girl tripped, and both she and the little dog she was carrying sprawled on the ground.

Angus pulled up when the girl started to cry. Tears coursed down her chubby cheeks as she sat up, leaves tangled in her amazing hair. But her next thoughts weren't for herself. She reached for the puppy, which had rolled free of her grasp.

"Peter," she sniffed brokenly. "Peter?"

Her brother slid to his knees on the ground next to her. "Renee? Are you hurt?" he demanded.

"I—I'm okay," she hiccuped. "It's—it's…" The little dog lay motionless on the ground, a blond heap of cocker pup. "Oh, David!" she wailed. "I've killed Peter!" Then she really started to cry—great, heart-rending sobs that reached even Angus's stony heart.

"Let me see," the man said gruffly. "Maybe he's just knocked himself out."

David started to hit at him then, striking out in anger and fear. "It's all your fault! You chased us!"

Angus fended off the flailing blows with one hand, then caught hold of the boy's arms and held him out of reach. "Stop it, boy," he ordered. "This isn't helping your pup."

David's thrashing stopped and Angus bent back over the little dog. As usual, he sneezed. Yet he reached out and felt its chest for a heartbeat. "He isn't dead," he said after a moment.

The little girl hiccupped again. "He's not?"

"No. I felt his heart beat. And he's breathing. Here, feel for yourself."

David came to kneel at his side and reached out just as Angus had, his fingers pressing the little dog's ribs. "He's telling the truth, Renee. Peter's alive!"

"Oh, thank goodness…thank goodness!" the little girl cried. Then she paused, still looking at Angus. "But he's not awake."

"We need to get him to Dr. Phelps," David said urgently.

The girl groaned. "How can we do that? Mommy and Daddy have the car, and Matt's at football practice!"

"Dr. Phelps has a van," David said.

"We can call him," Renee agreed.

Angus stood up and wiped his nose with his hankie. "Where is this Dr. Phelps? In town?"

Both children nodded. They looked at him with huge, hopeful eyes.

Generosity wasn't a part of Angus's nature. But a hurt animal was more than even he could resist. Whenever he saw one, he thought of Bossy the cow and Andy the goat, and he was swept back to a time in his childhood when they'd been his only friends. "All right, get in the car," he said gruffly. "I'll take you."

The children looked at each other. It was obvious they'd been told never to go anywhere with a stranger. But the situation was such that David said, "It'll be okay. We have to do something to help Peter. Okay, mister, you can take us."

Angus raised an eyebrow at his concessionary tone, but said nothing. He helped the children pick up the little dog and carry him to the car, then he drove them all into town.

Once David had directed him to the vet's office, Angus carried the dog inside. The little piece of yellow fur had started to come around. He was awake now, but he wasn't moving much.

The plump woman at the reception desk hurried to open the door that led to the rear examination rooms.

Dr. Phelps, wearing a white lab coat, came immediately. After learning what had happened, he told them. "At first blush, I'd say he's probably okay. But I'd like to check a little more. Why don't you go sit in the waiting room? It'll be a few minutes."

When he'd talked to the children, his voice had been warm. When he turned to Angus, it cooled. "I take it, since you caused the accident, you're going to be good for the cost?"

"Yeah," Angus conceded. "I'll pay."

The three of them settled in the waiting area, the silence broken only by Angus's frequent sneezes.

"Maybe we should call Mom and Dad," David said.

"Maybe we should wait and see how the dog is," Angus suggested.

A woman arrived for her appointment, her cat in a carrier. She smiled broadly when she saw Angus.

"Mr. Watson! Hello. I never expected to see you again so soon. And here, of all places. I didn't know you had a pet."

Angus moved uncomfortably in his seat, nodding at Marion Clark, the real-estate agent who'd been paying periodic calls to the farm under the guise of friendly interest. At first, Angus had suspected her of being suspicious of him; then he'd realized—rather incredulously—that her goal was to interest him! "Ah, it's not me. I don't have a pet. It's, ah, the kids here." He motioned to Renee and David.

"You know Mr. Stump?" Renee asked, keeping up their pretense even in her worry. She kicked her feet under her chair and her hands were restless. She wouldn't relax until she knew the fate of her dog.

"Mr. Stump?" the woman repeated.

Angus shrugged dismissal. "She's a child. She gets names mixed up."

"But that's your—"

Angus interrupted the little girl's treble. "Miss Clark has been very kindly making me feel welcome in the community."

Marion Clark's eyelids fluttered and she patted her

strawberry-blond hair. "I feel responsible since I'm the one you trusted to find you a comfortable home."

Angus smiled tightly. "Well, as I've said before, the farmhouse couldn't be better for my purposes."

The woman dimpled and glanced at the children. "I told you you'd enjoy your neighbors. The Marshacks are a wonderful family—especially these two." Her smile faded when she finally sensed the children's worry. "Has something bad happened to one of your pets?" she asked them.

Renee started to answer, but Angus cut her off again. "Her puppy had an accident," he said. "We brought him straight in."

"Oh, dear," the woman sympathized.

Angus sneezed hugely. As time passed his allergies were getting worse. The last place on earth he wanted to be at that moment—at any moment!—was a veterinarian's office, where there were enough loose dog hairs floating around to keep him sneezing for a week!

"Do you have a problem with animal dander?" Marion Clark asked.

He nodded.

She rummaged in her purse. "I have an antihistamine right here with me. I'm allergic to cats myself, but I love my Snookems so much I can't stand the thought of not having her." She handed a tablet to Angus, who promptly took it. He swallowed it without water.

"You're very lucky to have Mr. Watson as a neighbor," she said to Renee and David. "Not everyone would be so willing to take time out of his busy day to help you with your pet.''

''But he's the one who…''

But Marion Clark had turned back to Angus. ''You fit right in in Tyler, Mr. Watson. I've heard more than one person say so. You know, if you think about it, this could be a nice place for you to put down roots.'' She paused. ''I have an idea! I'm hosting a little party tomorrow night…just a few friends getting together. Why don't you come, too? We'd love to have you join us. That is, if you—''

Angus was relieved when the doctor chose that moment to enter the waiting room. He was carrying Peter, who once again looked perky and alert. The puppy nearly wagged his tail off when he saw the children.

''Well,'' the doctor said, smiling, ''he seems to be fine. I don't think there are any broken bones or internal injures. All he did was bump his head and lose consciousness. But what I'd like to do is keep him overnight, just to be sure there's nothing more serious. Is that all right with you, Renee?''

''He's fine?'' Renee questioned, needing to hear the words of reassurance again.

''Perfectly fine as far as I can tell.''

''Can I give him a kiss?'' Renee asked. The doctor handed the dog to her, and she held the puppy tightly. ''I won't ever let anything hurt you again, Peter,'' she promised. ''Never, ever, ever!'' She kissed the little dog's head.

''I also called your parents, David. I thought they should know. They asked me to tell you to wait here for them." He turned to Angus. "They also asked me to deliver their thanks to you as well."

Angus had already glanced at the door. Far too much attention was being paid to him for his comfort.

Dr. Phelps followed his gaze. He said, "You can go after you settle up with Fiona."

The plump woman was back behind the counter. She handed him an itemized invoice. When Angus got to the total his eyes widened, but he dutifully dug into his wallet and paid cash.

"Thanks, doc," he mumbled, then bolted for the door.

"Mr. Watson?" Marion Clark called after him. "You won't forget the party tomorrow night, will you? I'll drop by to give you the address."

He shut the door behind him and stomped out to his car. This job was really beginning to get to him. First and foremost, he hadn't picked up any substantial new clues in several days, and Celeste Huntington was going to have a fit pretty soon! And second, he didn't like the way he was starting to feel about the inhabitants of this town, especially—to his great irritation—Marion Clark. The woman's persistence was beginning to pay off. Under other circumstances, he'd go to that party of hers, encourage her a little and see what happened. She wasn't bad-looking and she did seem willing.

But isn't that what had happened to Vic Estevez, his predecessor? The *missing* Vic Estevez? The Vic Estevez who'd gone soft and betrayed his employer because of a woman?

Had Vic been drawn in little by little, smile by

smile, greeting by greeting—so slowly that he'd barely noticed the town was starting to suck him in?

Angus shrugged his burly shoulders. Well, that wasn't going to happen to him! He was made of sterner stuff. When employers paid him, they got their money's worth. He never let himself get sidetracked.

The silver Buick was parked directly in front of the sign that read Animal Crackers. "Yeah," he muttered as he settled behind the wheel, "you're a real tough cookie. But if you're so tough, then what the hell are you doing in a place like this? Animal Crackers! Geeze!"

The cocker pup's leash had been forgotten on the seat in the children's hurry. Angus gathered it up, gave it a toss, and amazingly, it draped across the top of the sign.

"Harrumph!" He sniffed, then drove away.

CHAPTER THIRTEEN

GRACIE AVOIDED Roger over the next few days. If the phone rang, she didn't answer it. If he came to the door, she pretended not to be home. If he left a note, she read it but didn't respond.

She couldn't think straight when she was with him! And she didn't know how much longer she could bear up under the pressure. She had to be on her own for a time!

She would have avoided everyone else as well, except she had responsibilities. Some she could get out of, others she couldn't.

People were still looking at her oddly and whispering, breaking off when she came near. She weathered the ordeal as best she could, at times feeling her ears burn.

It was when she was visiting one of her shut-ins that she received her worst shock. Mrs. Olmsted, an elderly widow barely able to walk, peered at her through close-set gimlet eyes and croaked, "So! How does it feel to rob the cradle? I wish I could'a done that in my day. I tell ya, I'd've sure liked to. A boy-toy—that's what they're called, isn't it? At least that's what they call 'em on my soaps!"

Gracie had smiled tightly at the woman after her

initial shock had worn off. She had set up her meal, then stayed and talked—about other things!—before cleaning up after. *Boy-toy?* She hadn't heard the term before. But it didn't sound good, and she doubted Roger would appreciate it.

The only other person she talked to was her niece. Of course, Sheila thought she was completely out of her tiny mind…she'd used that exact colorful description. And Gracie was beginning to wonder herself.

Roger was personable, attractive, gainfully employed. He came from a good family, said he loved her *and* he wanted to marry her. And she was running away.

Maybe she *was* out of her mind!

The doorbell rang and Gracie froze.

"Aunt Gracie! It's me!" Sheila called through the crack. "Open the door and stop being silly. Honestly, this is so ridiculous!"

Gracie sidled up to the door. "Are you alone?" she asked.

"Just me and my shadow," Sheila retorted. Then, as she came inside, she started to hum and do a soft shoe to the familiar tune.

Gracie quickly closed the door, and Sheila collapsed on the couch, laughing.

Jo-Jo thought this was all great fun—more fun than he'd had the entire week. He bounced up and down on the couch, barking excitedly.

Once they got the poodle settled, Sheila gave Gracie a quick appraisal. "You look awful!" she exclaimed.

Gracie grimaced. "That's what family is for, isn't it? Brutal honesty."

Sheila leaned forward to touch Gracie's clasped hands. "I'm sorry. I didn't mean to be brutal. But you don't look very well. You have dark circles under your eyes and they're all puffy."

"Again, thanks."

"Oh, my. We are touchy!"

"Well, with compliments like that…"

"Your hair's a pretty color," Sheila offered. Then she said more soberly, "Why don't you talk to him, Aunt Grace? Put both of you out of your misery?"

When Gracie said nothing, Sheila sighed and changed the subject. "Would you like to hear the latest installment in the Angus Watson saga? Brick has decided it's time to call in reinforcements. He's done something positively ingenious! He's enlisted Annabelle Scanlon and her closest gossip cohorts to watch out for Celeste Huntington! He thinks she's about to make an appearance in Tyler! I don't know how or why, and he won't say, of course. Mysterious police ways, I suppose. But there it is. That's what he's done. He's turning a plague into a plus!"

In spite of herself, Gracie was interested. She seated herself in the chair. "Has he told them anything more than he's told us?"

"He seems to only tell people what they need to know. The rest he keeps to himself."

"Probably good police policy. Will Annabelle and the group be able to keep their mouths shut? Or doesn't he care if Angus Watson knows?"

"Oh, he cares. He's told Annabelle all about the

threat to Daphne's baby and how important it is that
Angus not hear a word of it. Annabelle is a busybody,
but she loves children—especially babies. She won't
do anything to ruin Brick's plans, whatever they are.
Neither will the others. You know,'' Sheila said upon
reflection, ''it's like Tyler is circling the wagons
against an outside force that's threatening one of our
own. We're not going to let them get away with it!
Only in this instance, instead of outlaws or hostile
Indians attacking, it'll be Celeste Huntington in a limousine!''

''A limousine?''

''She rich, isn't she?''

The room grew silent and Gracie's mind wandered.
She'd almost forgotten that Sheila was there until her
niece said softly, ''I should go.''

Gracie looked up, startled. She hadn't meant to be
rude. ''You don't have to,'' she said. ''It's all right.
I'm not—''

''Roger looks almost as bad as you do,'' Sheila
interrupted.

''You've seen him?'' Gracie asked, her heart leap-
ing at the mention of his name.

''At the square. He seemed…distracted.''

Gracie rubbed her arm and looked down at the
floor.

Sheila sighed again and stood. ''I really do have to
go. Especially since I'm not making any headway
here.''

Gracie's head jerked up. ''Did he send you to talk
to me?''

Sheilie smiled wryly. ''No, I'm here on my own,

Aunt Grace. All I forgot was my ball-peen hammer.''
At Gracie's blank look, she added, ''So I could use
it to bang some sense into your head!''

Gracie didn't know whether to laugh or to be offended.

Sheilie leaned forward to kiss her cheek. ''I'm sure
you'll make the right decision, Aunt Grace. Just don't
wait too long. Okay?''

Gracie hugged her niece and murmured something
soothing.

RAINE ATWOOD PAUSED to rub her back as she stood
at her kitchen counter making egg-salad sandwiches.
Her pregnancy had reached the point where each day
made a visible difference, and her dancer's body,
though still strong and supple, had lost a great deal
of its grace.

''I wish you'd let me help,'' Roger complained,
watching her work. ''I'm the one who should be waiting on you.''

''Gabe's been doing enough of that lately,'' she
said, grinning. ''I barely lift a finger when he's off
duty.''

''He wants to do all he can for you,'' Roger said.

''He always has,'' Raine replied. ''But I'm not
completely helpless. Here,'' she said, turning. She
handed him two plates with a diagonally cut sandwich
on each, plus a mound of potato chips and a pickle.

Roger waited until she'd chosen a place across the
table from him before he set the plates down.

She grinned again. ''I have to tell you, I'm really
going to be glad to get back to normal.''

Roger hadn't planned to visit Raine for lunch today. He'd been driving by and had stopped on a whim. Raine had been surprised, but welcomed him happily. Gabe was on a twenty-four-hour shift at the fire station.

Raine looked across at him as she chewed her first bite. Her green eyes were speculative. "So how's it going with Gracie Lawson?" she asked.

"Awful."

"Does she still think you think she's an irresponsible breeder? You haven't gotten past that yet?"

Roger pushed his plate away. Suddenly, he'd lost what little appetite he'd had. "We're way beyond that now."

"What is it then?" she asked, frowning.

Roger sat back. "Do you remember when you first came back to Tyler from New York and we had lunch at Timberlake Lodge? Shortly after you married Gabe?"

"The first time I married Gabe," she clarified. "Yes, I remember."

"And I told you then, when you asked, that I hadn't found the person I wanted to marry yet?"

She grew still. "I remember that, too."

"I have now. It's Gracie Lawson."

Raine stared at him. "You're that serious, then?"

"I'm afraid so. I love her. I love everything about her. Her feistiness, her independence, her determination, the soft look that comes into her eyes when she thinks no one's looking. Her smile, the way she loves animals—"

"I have heard a few people talk," Raine interrupted dryly.

"So have I. So has Gracie." He picked at his potato chips, breaking one or two. "She thinks I'm too young for her. She also thinks what I want is a fling!"

Raine took another bite of her sandwich before answering, then quickly apologized. "Sorry. I can't seem to get filled up! If I'm not careful, I'm going to double my weight in the last few weeks!" She pushed the plate away, as he had. "I have to regain control of myself," she said, then she studied him again, carefully. "Have you told her how you feel? Have you come right out and said it?"

"I've asked her to marry me!" he exclaimed.

"And that's when she said—"

"Exactly!" Roger shot to his feet and began to pace restlessly across the floor. "I don't know what more I can do, Raine. I can't seem to get through to her!"

Raine thought for a moment. "Have you thought that possibly she's afraid?"

"I *know* she's afraid. She had a really bad experience a couple of years ago. I'm not privy to the whole story, but I know it wasn't pretty."

"Well, that's it, then."

"But *I'm* not *him!*" Roger said in frustration, dropping back into his chair.

"Put yourself in her place, Roger. It takes a lot of nerve to open yourself up to the possibility of being hurt again, particularly when you've been hurt very badly before." She paused. "Would you like me to talk to her?"

Roger shook his head. "You have enough on your plate at the moment." He motioned to her protruding stomach.

Raine smiled. "No, I ate most of it," she quipped, showing him her nearly empty sandwich plate, "unlike someone else I know."

"I'll fix that right now," Roger grinned, and consumed the remainder of his sandwich in three or four bites. "You make a mean egg salad," he complimented her at the end.

"Thank you." She tipped her head. "When I married Gabe I only knew how to make a couple of dishes really well."

"The first or the second time?" he teased.

"Both!" she retorted, and they shared a friendly chuckle.

Roger got up to leave. "Thanks, Raine," he said.

"I didn't do anything," she insisted.

"You listened," he said, and squeezed her hand in appreciation.

After leaving Raine and Gabe's house, Roger was in a little better frame of mind. Yet he still didn't have a solution to his problem. How could he get Gracie to accept that he was serious and admit that she cared for him, too, when he couldn't even persuade her to talk to him?

Then it dawned on him that he'd already hit on the answer. He would take her away and *make* her listen.

The more Roger thought about it, the more firmly the plan became entrenched. If she wouldn't see him, wouldn't talk to him—and who knew how long she planned to carry this into the future—his only choice was to force the issue.

Roger began to formulate his plans. He got in touch with everyone he needed to contact; took care of all the contingencies he could think of; enlisted the special help of Fiona, Sheila and Matt Johnston, swearing them all to secrecy.

Finally, everything was ready.

GRACIE SAID GOODBYE to the boys and hurried out to the Miata. She jumped inside and, after the engine purred to life, backed quickly into the street.

She'd almost called and cancelled her volunteer work with the meals program for shut-ins today. Emotional havoc was starting to take a toll. Upon awakening, she'd felt ill. Her head ached, she had no energy, her throat was sore. But considering it, she realized all her symptoms could easily be related to stress. She was making herself sick by denying her true feelings.

She parked the car near the church and hurried toward the activity building. She wasn't looking forward to making her rounds. It was hard to pretend to be happy and upbeat when you were neither. When all you could think about was one man. How it would be to be married to him, to be his mate for life, to have his children—it was a possibility! She wasn't against having children, she'd just reconciled herself to the fact that she probably wouldn't. A baby... Her own baby... Hers and Roger's baby—

She was just about to enter the wide door when Roger appeared from nowhere and took hold of her arm. As always when they made contact, her heart broke into a rapid drumbeat. In the days since she'd last seen him, he'd grown even dearer to her. What was she thinking, she asked herself, keeping them apart? Wasn't a large measure of happiness tied to a person's willingness to take a chance? But realizing that and actually doing it were two very different things.

She tried to free her arm. "Roger—this isn't at all necessary! I—"

He said nothing. Instead, he scooped her up into his arms and started to carry her back to the parking lot.

"Roger!" she cried, shocked. "Roger, put me down! Put me down this instant!" She looked around to see who might be watching them. "We're—we're creating a scene!"

He passed the little red Miata and went two cars down to his Saturn. By this time Gracie was determined to put a stop to this lunacy. He was going to do it! Just as he had warned her he would, he was going to take her off somewhere and... And she didn't want it to be like that! She'd been wrong not to talk with him sooner. Wrong not to listen to him. Wrong to cut him off so completely.

"Roger...please!" she breathed. "I have something I want to tell you. Just listen...please."

He behaved as if he didn't hear her. He opened the driver's door, leaned inside and maneuvered her into the passenger seat.

Gracie gave an aggrieved yelp when she lightly thumped her head on the window glass.

Still he said nothing. He merely slid into the driver's seat and started the engine.

Before the car began to move, Gracie tried the door release.

"It's been disabled," he said, breaking his silence.

"Roger, I am *not* enjoying this!"

He turned to look at her and gave a little smile. "You aren't supposed to…yet."

"I—I'll scream!" she threatened.

He shrugged. "Go ahead."

Gracie tried to roll her window down, but it wouldn't budge.

"That's been disabled, too," he said.

Gracie jerked back into place and crossed her arms.

"Put your seat belt on," he directed.

"No."

He stopped the car at the entrance to the road and did it himself. She tried not to react when, from necessity, he touched her.

The car started off again and picked up speed.

"I want to go home," she said, and a little later repeated the demand.

He, of course, didn't answer either time.

They passed the Tyler town limits. As the car flashed by, she turned to see the Welcome to Tyler sign on the opposite side of the road.

"Roger, you just can't do this. Jacques and Jo-Jo…and what about Serra and your patients—"

"It's all been taken care of. Sheila's going to watch out for the boys and Fiona will take care of Serra. As for my patients, I'm officially on vacation for the next few days."

Gracie closed her eyes. "I can't believe Sheilie would be a party to something like this. And Fiona!"

"We have to talk, Gracie. And since you aren't willing to do it on your own—"

"So this is my fault?"

"You could say that. I'm not the one who barricaded myself in my house and wouldn't answer the telephone."

"I went out," she defended.

"Not anywhere I could see you."

Gracie had a good explanation. She'd even come around to his way of thinking—they did have to talk! But she wasn't going to tell him that while he was carrying things to such extremes.

She folded her arms again and stared out the window. She'd be darned if she'd say another word until he stopped the car. Which didn't seem to bother him at all, since he immediately started to hum a tune that she recognized as a favorite of hers, one that had been recorded years ago by Stevie Wonder.

CHAPTER FOURTEEN

GRACIE RECOGNIZED the area where Roger took her—Lake Geneva—since he made no attempt to hide their destination. The drive through the country had been beautiful, and at the resort, the hardwood trees were resplendent in their multitude of fall colors.

The car rolled to a stop in front of a rustic cabin on a hill overlooking the lake.

"What's this?" she asked, her first utterance since they'd left Tyler.

"My family's place," he said. "We've had it for years. Uncle Zachary bought it sometime in the twenties."

He opened his door and got out, then leaned inside to assist her.

"I'm not coming in," she said, hunkering down in her seat.

"Grace, don't be like this."

"I'm not!" she repeated stubbornly. "Anything we had to say could have been said in Tyler."

He sighed. "All right. If we have to, we'll do it the hard way." He undid the seat belt, scooped her back into his arms, then maneuvered her around the steering wheel and out of the car.

"I could scream right now and have you arrested," she threatened as he carried her to the front door.

"Uncle Zachary still keeps in touch with the police chief here, who once worked on the Tyler police force. When Uncle Zachary was chief, he took the guy under his wing and treated him like a son. Who do you think he would believe?"

"You've thought of everything, haven't you?"

"I tried," Roger quipped.

Hitching her up in his arms, he juggled with the keys, found the right one and finally stepped through the door.

Gracie had her first view of the interior of the cabin as she was carried over the threshold. It could easily have come from the pages of a how-to-have-a-great-looking-cabin-to-relax-and-spoil-yourself-in magazine. It was all rough timbers and paneling and quality-made furnishings that fit in with the rustic look. A huge stone fireplace filled one wall and an ornamental iron chandelier hung from the vaulted ceiling. But what immediately caught her eye was the gigantic grizzly bear—arms raised, long claws and teeth on permanent display—that stood in challenge to anyone who entered the room.

"My God," Gracie breathed.

Roger placed her on her feet and followed the direction of her wide gaze. "Oh," he said. "Grace, meet Ben...Ben, this is Gracie."

"It has a name?" she said incredulously.

Roger smiled. "He didn't until I gave him one when I was a little kid. You remember the television show about a bear, *Gentle Ben*, don't you?"

"I remember," Gracie murmured. That particular knowledge didn't help. This bear was still an intimidating sight. "Where—where did it come from? Did your uncle or your father—"

"—Shoot it?" He laughed. "No, Uncle Zachary got hold of it from some kind of seizure he made. It was part of a cache of stolen goods. When the case was over, the owner didn't want it anymore and Uncle Zachary said he had the perfect place for it. Damn thing used to scare me to death when I was little, until I named it."

Gracie remembered the earliest family photograph on his wall—the one where Roger was about ten. Was it during that time period that he'd named the bear?

She turned away, not wanting to think about it. Not wanting to think about him as a child.

She went to a window and looked out at the lake. He came up behind her. She could sense that he wanted to touch her, to take hold of her shoulders and pull her against him, but her stiffened back must have given him pause.

"I had to do this, Grace," he said quietly. "Don't be angry. It's the only way I could think to—"

She moved away from him. And when she was at a safe distance, she said, "All right, let's talk."

He considered her for a moment, then made a gesture that invited her to take a seat on the cinnamon-colored couch facing the fireplace. Gracie perched on the edge of a cushion. Roger remained standing.

He started to speak, but she cut him off. "Before you say anything," she said, lifting a hand, "you asked about Paul—about who he was, about what had happened." She took a breath. "As you probably gathered, Paul and I were in a long-term relationship. He's a handler. He specializes in sporting dogs, especially English setters. He takes them out hunting, lets them do what they're bred to do, and he takes them to shows. His record with his dogs is superb. He's got a list of champions that's longer than your arm. People clamor for his services." She paused. "We met about ten years ago, when I was just starting to have success with Jacques and Hortense. We became friends, kept seeing each other at shows, then eventually, our friendship changed into something more. It seemed so natural, so right. And everyone around us took it for granted, took us for granted. We were a couple in everyone's eyes. It was assumed that one day we'd marry. I know I—" She broke off.

Roger started to come to her, but Gracie again stopped him with a raised hand. "I have to say this, Roger. Please."

He held back, his body tense.

A tight smile flickered across her lips. "I assumed it, too," she continued. "Paul's base is in Oregon, so we didn't see each other as often as we'd have liked. Sometimes he'd be on one circuit, while I was on another. Sometimes we'd meet when neither of us had anything scheduled—we both had assistants to watch out for things when we were away." She paused again.

"Then, two years ago, he came to a show I was at and introduced everyone to his new wife, Jessica. She was a handler, too. Only she was just starting out.

She was nineteen—nineteen! Everyone knew her, but no one had suspected…"

Her voice broke, and Roger couldn't restrain himself any longer. He rushed over to take her in his arms. "Stop it, Gracie," he said from above her ear. "You don't have to say anything else."

Gracie wanted to melt against him, to forget everything but her need of him. She wanted to stop thinking about the past, stop talking about it! But the past would always be a part of her present until she exorcised it. "There's only a little more," she said.

Roger held her close. He wouldn't let go when she tried to pull away, so she continued speaking from where she was, her cheek pressed tightly against his shoulder. "It was horrible," she whispered huskily. "I heard the news from someone else before I heard it from Paul. He was too ashamed to talk to me alone. He never did, in fact. I never got to ask him why…"

The memory of those moments tore like a knife blade through Gracie's tender flesh. But if she was ever to heal, if she was ever to stop thinking of herself as "damaged," she had to face the pain.

"I never knew he was interested in anyone else," she said. "There was never any sign. Possibly… possibly it was something that happened so quickly he never had the chance. But he should have told me. He should have told me when we were alone and not…"

"Grace…Grace," Roger murmured softly, holding her even tighter. "I knew you'd been hurt. Badly hurt. But I had no idea… How could he do that to you?"

She shook her head, moisture glistening in her eyes. "I'm not totally sure he meant to."

Roger cupped her face in his hands. "No. Don't give him that, Grace. He shouldn't have an out. Not from you." He looked at her carefully. "Do you still love him? Is that why—"

She answered before he finished. "No. Not anymore."

"But it still hurts," he said quietly.

"Not as much as it used to. It was hard…going to other shows, having everyone feel sorry for me. So I stopped going. I…stopped everything, except raising my puppies. That's why I ended up selling the kennel. It wasn't because of Paul, like people thought! I sold it because I needed to…for myself!"

"And that's about the time I came along," he murmured wryly.

She nodded. "In an act of perfect timing."

Roger's nicely shaped mouth curved into a smile. "When I first saw you, I couldn't believe my eyes. I thought you'd gone out of my life forever when I was fourteen."

"When you were my bag boy," she murmured softly.

"I didn't consciously measure other women against you," he said, "but you were always there, in the back of my mind. I knew what I wanted, but I couldn't find it…because I couldn't find you."

Gracie's discipline broke. All the love that she'd been suppressing burst over her in a rush. She didn't care anymore about the fact that she was older, that some people might disapprove, or that Paul, when he heard, would jump to the same conclusion as others would—that she was with a younger man in order to spite him. He'd be wrong, just as they were. She kissed Roger, putting everything she felt into it.

"I love you, Grace," he said huskily, once their lips broke apart. "I've always loved you, and I always will. It's not going to go away."

"I think the reason I wouldn't admit... I was afraid that if you were only playing with me, I might die," she answered. "I couldn't enter into another relationship and have it fail. I had to be sure. I had to be sure that *you* were sure."

Chills went up and down Gracie's spine as Roger nuzzled the side of her neck. "I'm sure," he said. "I'm far surer than you are."

"I'm quite sure," she murmured.

"I haven't heard you say it."

"Say what?" she breathed, her head falling back as he continued to rain sweet kisses along the base of her throat.

"You know."

Gracie smiled. Freed from the past, she had the future to look forward to. *They* had the future. "I love you, Roger," she said earnestly. "I love you wholly, completely and with my entire heart."

With that confession, the time for talk drew to an end.

Roger stood up and held out a hand.

Gracie knew what he wanted. He wanted her to come with him of her own free will.

She reached out and, without hesitation, placed her hand in his.

GRACIE PADDED, in her socks, back to Roger. Night had fallen and the glow of burning wood in the fireplace guided her way. As she handed Roger his mug of soup, she glanced at the ever-present grizzly.

"I feel like I should have brought a third helping," she murmured.

Roger held her mug as she slipped back under the warm, feather-filled comforter that they'd spread onto the rug in front of the hearth.

Besides her socks, all Gracie wore was a long T-shirt of Roger's. He wasn't wearing anything at all.

Once she'd burrowed back against him, he glanced over his shoulder. "I don't think old Ben likes soup."

"You've asked him before?" she teased.

"He's a meat-and-potatoes kind of bear. *Rare* meat and potatoes."

Gracie took a sip from her mug. "Mmm," she murmured approvingly. Following the afternoon they'd shared, she was in need of nutrition.

"I'll say," Roger agreed, only instead of sipping his soup, he nuzzled the curve of her neck.

"Stop that!" She laughed, moving her head away, all the while protecting her soup. "I want to eat. I'm hungry."

"So am I." He grinned.

"Roger!"

He kissed her earlobe. "All right. I'll let you eat. It's in my best interests to keep up your strength."

"Insatiable beast!" she chided.

Roger adjusted his arm so that it curved comfortably around her as they sat, their backs propped against the cinnamon-colored couch.

An incredible sense of rightness and joy filled the room, a peace like neither of them had experienced before.

"Can you hear it?" Roger asked after a moment.

"Hear what?" Gracie breathed, listening.

"The universe. It's settling into place. There was a piece missing—us! And now we're together, as we should be."

"That's beautiful, Roger," she said, smiling.

"It's true."

She let her head rest against his shoulder, her mind going back over the afternoon. "I can't believe this has happened," she said softly. "I can't believe I resisted it for so long. I was really—"

"Uh-uh! No, you don't. Not a word of criticism against the woman I love."

"Even if she deserves it?" Gracie said.

"Everything happens in its own good time. Hasn't anyone ever told you that? And if it took some waiting to get to this—"

"I do love you, Roger," Gracie interrupted. "I love you so much I can't—I can't put it into words! It's just there, a part of me. I didn't expect it to happen. I didn't want it to happen, but it did!"

Rekindled passion flared in his eyes. He kissed her, drawing it out for a long, long time.

When they finally broke apart he murmured huskily, "Eat your soup. While you still have the chance."

"You, too," she returned breathlessly.

A falling log sent sparks up the chimney and lent the room an extra burst of light.

"How long can we stay here?" she asked after several moments.

"All I could arrange was a few days."

"I was really angry at first."

"Tell me about it."

"I was just about ready to tell you how wrong I was, and you took the initiative right out of my hands! Did you tell Sheilie and Fiona everything you planned?"

"I had to. They wouldn't have helped otherwise."

"Busybodies," Gracie grumbled in mock irritation.

"Angels," Roger decreed.

They looked at each other and laughed.

"What are your parents going to say about this?" Gracie asked. "I'm sure your mother won't—"

"My dad will clap me on the back and tell me what a lucky man I am. My mother? My mother will have to adjust."

"Were you able to work out whatever it was that was coming between your father and your sister?"

"My *mother* was coming between my father and my sister. And the answer is I tried. And maybe it helped a little. My dad called the other day and told me John—that's Missy's husband—had called and told him Missy said he could talk to the kids this Sunday. For fifteen minutes only, but that's better than it was before, when she wouldn't let them have any contact."

"It sounds as if you did some good."

Roger shrugged. "Maybe. If my mother keeps her promise."

"Seriously, do you think she'll try to come between us because I'm—"

"No, I won't let her. And she knows it."

Gracie finished her soup and slid the mug onto the low table nearby. Roger did the same.

"Do you see any reason why we should wait to get married?" he asked when she'd settled back against him.

"Not a reason in the world," she said.

"Do you want a big wedding? Gown? Church?"

Gracie shook her head. "I'll marry you tomorrow, if you want. In what I wore today."

His cheeks creased into a wide smile. "Good, then let's do it!"

Gracie looked at him. "Do you mean it?"

"I've never meant anything more in my life. And you won't have to wear the same clothes. Sheila packed a bag."

Gracie started to smile. "You mean…this isn't a kidnapping, it's an elopement?"

"Why not?" Roger said, laughing.

Gracie threw her arms around his neck and pressed herself against him. She loved the way his body looked and felt—wonderfully, masculinely beautiful, with long, nicely constructed muscles that were smooth to the touch and hard underneath. But mostly, she loved the person inside. The man who was so sensitive and so strong in the most meaningful sense of both words.

"Yes, why not?" she echoed.

His arms folded her close and slowly, as they

kissed, they moved away from the couch to lie on the floor.

Light flickered from the fire, bathing them in gold.

"Roger, wait!" Gracie said suddenly, pushing away from him. "The boys! Serra!"

He frowned, not understanding. "Are being cared for. Sheila…Fiona…"

"I mean, how are they going to get along? We're going to move in with you, right? You'll want to stay living above the clinic? The boys will be fine with that, but do you think Serra will accept them? We'll be like invaders in her world. And she's already been through so much. I wouldn't want to—"

"Serra already likes you."

"But the boys! She's never met—"

"Grace. Lovely Grace," he said warmly. "You worry far too much. We'll introduce them slowly, let them take their time. Serra isn't afraid of other dogs as much as she's afraid of people. Jacques and Jo-Jo are sweet and friendly. They'll all be fine."

Gracie tilted her head and looked at him. "You know?" she said consideringly. "Fiona's right. You are good. Maybe I will change vets."

Then she broke into a fit of giggles as he started to tickle her.

"Is that all I am—good?" he demanded. "I'll show you *good!*" Then he stopped tickling her and moved onto other, much more satisfying areas of endeavor.

In her remaining seconds of clarity, Gracie had another thought. This time, about the direction of her life: hadn't it taken a nice turn?

HOMETOWN REUNION

continues with

Hot Pursuit

by Muriel Jensen

Here's a preview!

HOT PURSUIT

THE CADILLAC hood ornament caught Rob Friedman's eye first. Then he saw the silver-gray body, so highly polished that it reflected the trees at the side of the road when the driver turned onto Main Street. The lines were long and sleek. The limo bore Illinois plates in the Airport Rental frame.

Rob's heart thumped against his ribs. It was her! Celeste Huntington, Daphne's mother-in-law. He'd known it was just a matter of time before she grew tired of waiting and came to Tyler herself, since her "spy"—the man she'd hired to observe Judy in the hope of learning Daphne's whereabouts—hadn't turned up a single clue.

"Sheriff's Dispatch," a courteous voice announced from the cell phone still cradled on Rob's shoulder.

"Give me Brick," he demanded, dealing the steering wheel another blow and taking hold of the phone.

"I'm sorry, he's out of the office at the moment. What's the nature of your—"

"It's an emergency!" he interrupted. "Patch me through, wherever he is!"

K. J. EBER BLINKED. A limo in Tyler? Whoa!

Then the truth came to him in a flash of understand-

ing: it was her. It had to be. Rob had said to be on
the lookout for any sign of the rich broad he was sure
would be coming to see Judy Lowery. He needed an
extra pair of eyes to help watch for signs of trouble,
he'd explained, so he'd shared with K.J. information
that only the Marshacks, Brick Bauer and Judy knew
about Daphne Sullivan and her daughter, and about
Vic Estevez's disappearance.

K.J. didn't know all the details, but the old broad
was after her granddaughter, who was hiding out with
the woman's daughter-in-law and some guy she'd
hired to find them. But the detective had turned on
her and taken the pair away instead. Rob and Brick
had helped them get away.

To cover for Daphne and Vic, Judy was telling anyone who asked that Vic had proposed marriage and
taken Daphne and her daughter Jenny to Santa Barbara to meet his family.

The limo was heading for Judy's.

K.J.'s heart began to thump. He ran the half block
back to the Hair Affair and asked breathlessly to use
their phone. But Rob's cell-phone number was busy.

All right, K.J. told himself. *Stay calm.* Rob, who
was half ice, was always telling him to stay calm; that
panic stalled your brain.

If this was indeed Celeste Huntington, she'd want
to know what Judy knew. And Rob had made it pretty
clear that the woman was ruthless. K.J. had to get
help for Judy, but he didn't have time to call the sheriff.

He started running toward Judy's house, his plan

of action not clearly formed in his mind. Physical confrontation wasn't his best thing.

But Rob would hate it if he missed this story. And if somebody didn't help Judy, the story might turn out to be her obit.

READER SERVICE™

The best romantic fiction direct to your door

Our guarantee to you...

The Reader Service involves you in no obligation to purchase, and is truly a service to you!

There are many extra benefits including a free monthly Newsletter with author interviews, book previews and much more.

Your books are sent direct to your door on 14 days no obligation home approval.

We offer huge discounts on selected books exclusively for subscribers.

Plus, we have a dedicated Customer Care team on hand to answer all your queries on
(UK) 020 8288 2888
(Ireland) 01 278 2062.